STEALING HEAVEN

STEALING
HEAVEN

ELIZABETH
SCOTT

HARPER TEEN
An Imprint of HarperCollinsPublishers

Stealing Heaven
Copyright © 2008 by Elizabeth Spencer

Library of Congress Cataloging-in-Publication Data is available.
ISBN 978-0-06-112280-4 (trade bdg.) — ISBN 978-0-06-112281-1 (lib. bdg.)

Typography by Jennifer Heuer
1 2 3 4 5 6 7 8 9 10
❖

First Edition

YF
sco

b18171266

ACKNOWLEDGMENTS

Thanks to Tara Weikum for her dedication, kindness, and belief in my work—you've been in my corner since the beginning, and I am so grateful for everything you do; and to Robin Rue, for continually proving that she's the best agent around.

Thanks also go to Katharine Beutner, Jessica Brearton, Clara Jaeckel, Shana Jones, Susie LeBlanc, Amy Pascale, Donna Randa-Gomez, Nephele Tempest, Marianna Volokitina, and Janel Winter for reading drafts, encouragement, and all-around support as I was writing this book.

Special thanks to my husband for believing in me and being the best man I know.

STEALING
HEAVEN

1

My first memory is staring through a window into a house that isn't mine. I'm not very old, three or four at the most, and a hand rests on my head and fingers tap twice softly on my left ear. I know this means I must be extra super quiet and wait exactly where I am. I am good at being quiet. I am good at waiting.

The window opens. Through it I see a carpet. It's all different colors and enormous, stretching out as far as I can see. I stare at it for a long time and then I hear a bag fall, clinking softly as it lands. I am scooped up in a pair of arms and held tight, the only sound the rhythmic slap of feet hitting the ground over and over again.

My name is Danielle. I'm eighteen. I've been stealing things for as long as I can remember.

My first memory is of the Lanaheim house, which I guess everyone has heard of, what with the Lanaheims being, well, who they are. It's not someone's home anymore, it's a museum, and we went there again today, toured the house.

Mom wanted to see what had happened to the place, and we didn't have anywhere we had to be since we'd just finished up in Charleston, so we went. She spent a lot of time talking to the tour guide, asking if Baltimore really is as awful as everyone says and was it true that once someone broke in and stole a lot of jewelry but left a diamond necklace sitting right out in the open on Mrs. Lanaheim's dressing room table?

The tour guide laughed and told Mom yes, it was true, and then led us into a big open room, which he called a "formal dining room," and started telling a story about daring thieves who were never caught. I didn't listen, just stood staring at the carpet. It looked so much smaller than I remembered.

I stared at it until Mom's bright voice called out, "Helen, sweetie, come and take a look at this—what is this again? A highboy? What's it used for? Oh, storing dishes and silver. Well, that makes sense, what with there being plates in there. Goodness, they sure are pretty. Helen, don't you think they're pretty?"

I don't think I need to tell you Mom knows exactly what a highboy is, right? What she really wanted was to stand next to something she'd passed by a long time ago, to know she was somewhere she'd been before and could easily come again.

She's laughing about it when we pull onto the interstate, talking about that and how the famed diamond necklace wasn't all that great because the center stone had a huge crack in it. "Funny how the guide forgot to mention that, isn't it?"

"I remember the carpet," I tell her. "It looked so much smaller than I thought it was."

"Well," she says, and glances over at me. "You've grown up. Helen."

"Very funny," I tell her. "I think you pick the most awful names you can to torture me."

She laughs. "Next place, you can be Sydney. Better?"

"Better. When will we get there?"

"Pass me a soda, will you, baby? No, not a regular one. Diet, and none of that 'oh, it's full of chemicals' stuff, okay?"

"Fine." I hand her a soda from the now-warm six-pack we got the last time we stopped for gas, and then stare out the window. I want to ask where we're going but I know she won't tell me. A good thief never tells anyone, even family, everything, but sometimes I wish Mom would break her own rules a little and trust me.

When we were in Charleston, I got to chatting with a server when Mom and I talked our way into a charity dinner in one of the houses we'd targeted. I remember the server told me she'd taken the job because she couldn't bear the thought of going home for the summer, that her mom drove her crazy by always wanting to know where she was going and who she was with. I laughed and said I totally understood.

I wondered if that's how Mom feels about me.

* * *

We end up in Aberwyn, Pennsylvania, which is full of very wealthy people living in very huge and very old houses. There's a whole string of towns like it lined up in a row right outside Philadelphia, and I've seen most of them. Mom and I have even been to Aberwyn before, but not for a couple of years. Mom will come back to the same place twice sometimes, but she usually likes to wait awhile before we return.

Right now, I'm already more than sorry we came back, as I'm currently stuck in Mr. and Mrs. William Henderson IV's kitchen window, being watched by the family dogs.

You'd think alarms would be our biggest worry, but they aren't. The thing is, alarm trips are usually accidents, malfunctions, or someone unable to punch their code in on time, and so most companies call the house first and then, if there isn't an answer, call the police. And the police usually take forever because they hate wasting their time as much as anyone else. We try really hard not to set off alarms, but the few times we have, we've been long gone with what we came for before anyone showed up.

The other thing is that most alarms are pieces of

crap. The companies come in and razzle-dazzle you, but nine times out of ten what you end up buying is something that will go off if a door is opened and maybe some motion sensors for the basement. Mom dated a guy who worked for an alarm company once. "Cheap, boring, and stupid," she always says about him, "but baby, did he know alarms."

Thanks to him, we know most people buy the cheapest alarm they can and pick codes they can easily remember. You'd be amazed how many we've turned off just by pressing "1" five, six, or seven times. Better yet, we also learned that a lot of people don't bother turning on their alarm during the day, figure it's light out and the neighborhood is safe, so what could possibly happen?

Dogs, on the other hand, are trickier. I'm usually able to deal with them, but there have been a few times—four, in fact—when I haven't. I once got bitten by a poodle (they make surprisingly good guard dogs) so bad I still have a scar on my arm. The other three times I was able to get out before anything happened, but all four of those houses were ones we didn't get anything from and sure as hell didn't visit again.

These dogs look okay though. I watched them as I pried the window open, and even though I woke them up, their barks were halfhearted and sleepy. Plus, it's obvious from the mangled shoes on the floor that these dogs haven't been trained to do much of anything.

The window, however, is a bitch. It wasn't locked, which was great, but as I was pushing myself through, it became real clear that it was either put in for appearances or during a time when people were a little smaller than they are now. The dogs have come over to investigate, and I croon to them as I wiggle my hips and tell myself to focus, to stay calm.

That's the thing about dogs. They can smell worry and fear, and if they do, it always sets them off. Right now I'm just a strange wiggling thing for them to sniff, and I need it to stay that way.

"You're very pretty," I tell one of them, a golden retriever who wags her tail and goes over to her food dish and picks it up, then drops it on the floor. If I could just get my ass through this window, I could find dog food, feed her, and have the run of the house.

The other dog isn't quite as accepting. Her tail is

wagging a little, but the fur on her back is raised and when I finally—finally!—push myself through the window and land on the floor, she growls. I lie perfectly still and wait while she sniffs me, making sure to avoid direct eye contact, which can be taken as a challenge. After a moment she gets bored and flops on the floor, yawning.

"Good dog," I tell her, and very slowly sit up. The retriever picks up her food dish and drops it again.

"Where's your food?" I whisper, and her tail wags very energetically, the other dog's ears perking up as well. Good. I look at my watch. I need to keep them distracted for ten minutes in case Mom has any problems.

I feed the dogs, then turn on the dishwasher and the faucet to drown out any noises Mom might be making that the dogs could hear. I don't hear anything except their very energetic eating, and so ten minutes later I turn the dishwasher off, refill the dogs' water bowls, and go back out the window, closing it as soon as I'm out. One of the dogs has her nose pressed against the glass, and I wave good-bye. Stupid, I know, but I can't help myself.

I wish I had a dog. I wish I had a place I could

come back to every day and call my own. I turn away and strip off my gloves, stuff them in my pocket, and then walk to the car, which we've parked a couple of blocks over. I drive back to the house, turn down the side street that runs parallel to the backyard. Mom is waiting. I pop the trunk, see her smile at me in the rearview mirror after she closes it.

"Go," she says when she gets in the car, and I do.

3

We take turns driving until we hit North Carolina and our storage place. We keep everything in a rental facility, the kind of place where people store old furniture and mildewed knickknacks and who knows what else. We park the car a mile away and walk through scrubby trees and weeds that skirt the edge of a couple of crappy subdivisions until we get there and then jimmy open the unit we've been borrowing.

Mom did some checking, back when we started coming here, and everything in it belongs to an old lady who died ten years ago and whose kids can't or won't deal with coming down and picking through it. There's a lot of stuff, but none of it is worth anything (we checked, ages ago) and so I guess I can see why no one would want to go through it. But it kind of sucks, doesn't it, that a person's whole life can be boiled down to a few things stuck in a room no one ever uses?

"I swear, this crap gets uglier every time," Mom says. "I'm going to have nightmares about the sofa."

It is pretty ugly, a big flower print with freaky green and yellow knitted things on the armrests. Plus all the cushions are shiny, worn from use. That's something I don't see much. Most of the houses I'm in, the furniture looks like it's never been sat on. I think it's nice that people once used this sofa, spent hours there talking or watching television. It seems cozy.

"Baby," Mom says, waving a hand in front of my face. "Help me sort, will you?"

I sit down next to her, pull on my gloves, and start picking through what she's spread out on the floor. A couple of pieces are crap, plate or new stuff, but the main set is from the early 1800s and is complete right down to the six zillion forks that people apparently needed to eat then. I don't feel like looking at any of it. I keep thinking about the sofa and the stupid knitted things on it, wondering what it must be like to call something yours and know it really is.

"What's going on in there?" Mom asks, leaning

over and kissing the side of my head.

I look at her. She's turning a sugar bowl around in her hands, running her fingers along the pattern etched on its sides.

"I was just thinking about the sofa."

"It really is awful, isn't it?" She laughs. "Oh hell, this sugar bowl is a replacement piece. Look—" She breaks off, glances at me. "You okay?"

"It must be nice to be able to say something's yours, you know? To be able to—"

"Baby, no one wants to call anything like this crap theirs. That's why it's in here." Mom puts the sugar bowl down, reaches out, and wraps her arms around me. "We'll be somewhere nice real soon, I promise. And when we are, you'll be able to look around and know everything there is ours for as long as we want it to be. How many people get that? I'll tell you. Not many. Instead they get stuck with"—she points at the sofa—"for their whole lives. We can go where we want whenever we want. We're lucky, baby. You know that, right?"

"I know," I say, and when she smiles at me I find myself thinking about Dad.

Dad introduced Mom to all of this. What we do,

I mean. She was a high-school dropout working as a waitress and shoplifting on the side when they met. He told her how stupid shoplifting was, pointed out that stores are always eager to make an example out of someone. He said he knew she could do better and introduced her to the fine art of burglary.

When I came along, Dad worked by himself until Mom got bored. Then they started bringing me with them. Babysitters were out of the question, obviously, and I was a quiet kid, the kind who could be left outside a house and who would stare, mesmerized, at a carpet. Mom says that's because this life was made for me, but I think it's just that this is all I've ever known.

Dad got arrested when I was five. We'd split up after hitting a series of houses right outside Princeton, Dad to stash the jewels—the rich like having woods around their houses, which has always worked to our advantage—and Mom and me to head back to the car and drive down to Trenton, where we'd meet up with Dad. Only it didn't work out that way because Dad never showed. I fell asleep waiting for him and the next thing I knew, Mom was carrying me out to the car and we were leaving town.

Dad got arrested walking out of the woods, and

that was it. Nothing we could do, nothing he could do, nothing his fancy lawyer could do. The police never found the jewels but they found all his gear and got a partial heel print from one of his shoes, and that was enough to send him to prison. That was the last I heard from him till I was nine, and by then he'd been out of prison for two years.

I suppose "out of prison" makes it sound like he was released, and that isn't technically true. He actually broke out of jail when I was seven and lives in—well, I don't know anymore. It used to be right outside Kansas City but now . . . he could be anywhere.

I never really got to know him. I saw him some when I was younger, when Mom took on a tough job. Back then, a getaway was easier without me around, and Dad owed her for—well, for making it so it was just her and me. He always sent me back to her as soon as he could, and when I did see him we spent most of our time sitting around his condo, which was pretty much as dull as it sounds. He got the jewelry from Princeton, of course, and it was enough for him to live on. I complained once, when I was eleven, about how we never went anywhere, and he said he wasn't going back to prison for anyone, even me. He was nice enough about it, but I got the message.

The last time I saw him he said all this stuff about knowing I could take care of myself, talked and talked and looked right through me, and the next time I tried to get in touch with him he was gone. Mom was silent for a long time and then she put her arms around me and asked how I was. She said I should be mad. I said I was, but the truth is I wasn't. I just wished he'd said good-bye. I wished he'd loved me enough to say that one word. I wished he'd thought I was worth it.

Mom and I are back on the road less than four hours later, heading north again. We stop in a suburb outside DC to spend the night, and the next day we rent another car and then visit a couple of places to read the Pennsylvania papers. Well, I read the papers. Mom reads magazines. She never cares about the news unless there's a mention of how daring we are or there's a hint the police might have some idea who they're looking for.

I only find two articles: a short one, just a few sentences about what was stolen, and a slightly longer one where Mrs. Henderson says that things would have been different if the family's beloved attack dogs hadn't been at the vet's for the day. I laugh about that until Mom gives me a look. I'm not supposed to do anything that will call attention to myself unless we need a distraction.

Not that I'm very good at making them. Distractions, I mean. Mom is, but that's because she's gorgeous. She's got really dark hair that always looks perfect and she has lots of curves. I'm like a very pale copy of her, my hair not as dark or as shiny, my curves a lot less curvy.

I look over at her. We're back in the car now because she's decided we're going shopping. She's singing along with the radio as we drive through a mall parking lot. I wonder what she looked like when she was eighteen. She probably caused car wrecks.

"What did you look like when you were my age?"

"What?" she says, distracted as she waves to someone who is—of course—letting her take his parking space.

"Nothing," I mutter. "I just wish I was pretty."

"Oh baby," Mom says. "You are pretty."

"No, I'm not."

"You are." Mom pulls into the parking space, turns off the car.

"I'm not."

"Danielle," Mom says, and I can tell she's angry. She never uses my name unless she's angry. "Will you please ask yourself if this is what we want to be doing right now?"

"It's what I want to do right now."

"Fine," Mom says, and looks at me. "Are you pretty right now? No, because what you are right now is a pain in the ass."

"Thanks a lot."

"Look, we're here to go shopping. There are things we need to get." She reaches over and gently nudges my arm. "New clothes for someone . . ."

"So I'll be a pain in the ass in new clothes."

"Baby, quit it. We're gonna go in there"—she points at the mall—"and you're gonna be able to get whatever you want. What's better than that?" She opens her car door. "Come on. Anything you want."

"All right." I sigh and get out of the car. Mom grins at me and loops her arm through mine as we walk.

When we're done at the mall we hit the road again, the latest and greatest from the magazines Mom read earlier stashed in the trunk. Traffic is awful, and I

look out the window, watch as we slowly pass a convenience store and a strip mall. An apartment com-
plex is next, then a church of some kind. It has a sign
that asks, WHAT DO YOU BELIEVE IN?

Mom snorts at that. "Anything I can hold in my
hands. No, better yet, anything I can sell." It's what
she always says when we pass signs like this. I look
over at her and she winks at me.

I wink back and she smiles, pats my knee. "So
how do you feel about the beach?"

My mother tells people she's sorry all the time.
She never means it, of course. But this, this hint of
what's to come—I know what it means. It's a little
gift from her to me, a way to make up for calling me
a pain in the ass before, and I smile back at her.

"It sounds good," I tell her. "It sounds great."

4

Now I know people think that thieves, when they hear the word "beach," head straight for Long Island or Cape Cod or Newport, but the thing is, those places are where the police expect you to go and so—well, it's obvious, right?

Plus the rich—the real rich, the rich that have had money for so long they'd probably bleed gold if you cut them—they have other places by the sea. Out of the way places. Places like Heaven.

I laugh when Mom passes me a map and taps a finger against it because places called Heaven are usually filled with boarded-up houses or worse, dippy types who own bed-and-breakfasts adored by other dips.

"I know," she says with a smile, "but trust me. This place will live up to its name. I can feel it."

She always can.

We pass through a tiny town called West Hill and then reach the beach. It's much smaller than I thought it would be: one public beach, a couple of private ones, and a one-street tourist strip filled with local places. There isn't even one chain restaurant. I've never seen anything like it. I'm used to beach towns full of sprawl and noise and places to hide.

I look over at Mom. She's grinning. "Hard to believe places like this are still around. And just wait, it'll get better."

I sure hope so because the beach houses we've passed are very small and obviously rentals. We drive down a bunch of narrow roads—a good sign— pass a few more tiny houses and a volunteer fire department, and then turn a corner. The second we do, I hear Mom suck in a breath.

In front of us is a wide, green, and very well-kept lawn, the gentle slope of a hill. At the top of the hill, hidden by landscaped boulders and trees, is a house. An old house. A huge house. Our kind of house.

There's lots more of them. We pass a country club with a very small and tasteful sign, the kind of place that is definitely never open to the public, and then there are homes everywhere, all very old and very well preserved.

Every single one is worth a second look, and then we are winding our way down into another town.

Heaven, a cutesy but not tacky sign proclaims, and though there's another tourist strip—even smaller than the first one we passed, and definitely more moneyed—the main attraction is the houses. We must pass a dozen, each one larger and older than the one before, and all of them practically screaming, "Money! Lots of money!"

"Wow," I say, and Mom laughs, smacks the steering wheel with one hand.

"This is even better than I thought it would be. It's . . ." She pauses, stares at a huge house perched on a cliff right by the ocean. "This is perfect. Hell, we won't even have to run title searches. These places . . ." She slows down as we drive by another home.

It's three stories, probably at least twenty-five rooms, and sits just waiting for us, the security gate propped open with a brick. A brick! On the lawn three blond children run around shrieking while a tired-looking Asian woman sits in the grass watching them. Two older kids climb into a huge sports utility vehicle and barely miss a group of cleaning people as they drive off.

And what are the cleaning people doing outside? Standing around a table that's clearly been set up for a party. And they're polishing silver. A whole table-ful of it.

"Oh baby," Mom says. "We're going to be very happy here."

There's an inn in Heaven, but it's smack in the middle of the tiny tourist strip and way too obvious. We drive back to West Hill and Mom finds two real estate offices. She picks the second one because it's a little shabby-looking, the kind of place where they're more than happy to take your money without asking many questions.

I take a walk while she's doing her thing and she finds me as I'm heading back to the car. "This town really is small," she says with a slight frown, and I nod. It is, and that's a definite downside to being here because if Mom asks me to meet anyone, avoiding them when it's time to drop out of sight could be a problem.

"Still, there's lots of summer people here," she says, "so that'll be a help. New faces around all the time and everything. Plus, we're all set to move in."

She waves a set of keys at me.

The house she's gotten us is outside West Hill, on the edge of a much poorer town. This is the kind of place I know well, the kind of place where people keep to themselves and keep their mouths shut.

The house is okay, I guess. It's furnished, but everything is old and crappy-looking. And the bathrooms are awful: one is bright green, and the other is, for some bizarre reason, dark pink.

"Ugh," I say, and close the pink bathroom door.

"We'll move somewhere nicer soon," Mom says. "But for now, while we're getting a feel for the place, this is good. Plus I got a great deal."

"How great?"

Mom grins and tells me about Sharon, the person she talked to at the real estate office. Sharon was desperate, an overworked woman with three kids, two divorces, and a—Mom makes a drinking motion.

"Didn't even look at the paperwork I filled out," she says. "I don't think she noticed much of anything other than the fact I was willing to pay a month's advance rent plus a security deposit in cash." She chuckles. "Plus she kept grousing about this other place, one that's got 'all the good beach rentals.' So now we know where to go when it's time for that."

We bring the rest of our stuff in—the important stuff—when it's dark, and then celebrate by going to a nearby casino. Well, Mom celebrates by doing that. She says I should come, but I can tell from her face she needs to blow off some steam and I've seen her making out with guys she's just met plenty of times. I drive her out there, tell her to be careful.

"Baby, I always am," she says, and kisses my cheek before sliding out of the car.

I drive back and unpack everything, then realize there's nothing to eat. Figures. Mom never thinks about stuff like that. We've each got ten pairs of new shoes from our earlier trip to the mall (we'll have to ditch them at some point, but for now they're all ours) but no food, no laundry detergent, and—after a check of the pink bathroom—no toilet paper.

I drive around looking for a supermarket but don't find one, just a bunch of bars. So I head back into West Hill and go to the one supermarket, which is just past a weird traffic circle thing that marks the middle of town.

It doesn't take long to get everything. Mom eats nothing but frozen food for whatever diet is currently popular, never mind that it's full of chemicals that will preserve her from the inside out, so getting her stuff is easy. I grab some real food for myself and then stop at the seafood case and look at the shrimp. I like shrimp but they really look gross. I didn't realize they were gray before you cooked them.

Plus, now that I think about it, I don't have a pot to cook them in. I look over at the lobsters. They're just sort of lying in a big display case of murky water, their claws bound with bright blue rubber bands.

"They'll steam one for you if you want."

I look over and see a guy standing next to me, motioning at the woman who's working behind the counter. "You got any mussels back there?" he asks when she looks at him. She rolls her eyes but turns around and heads into the back.

"Seriously," he says after she goes, glancing over at me. "It doesn't even take that long. And I know the guy who catches them, so I promise they're good."

"Uh huh," I say. A local. A local with bad hair, what was once a buzz cut grown out enough to be at the stage where it can't be combed into any sort of style. It's just sort of everywhere. He probably spends his free time sitting around drinking beer and plotting ways to date his cousins. I look back at the lobsters.

"Okay, so I don't really know who brings them in. I just feel bad for the guys. I mean, look at the water they're stuck in. Who'd want to swim around in that all day?"

I look over at him again. Nice green eyes. And I was just thinking the same thing about the lobsters myself. But still. "So why don't you get one?"

"I spent a summer working on a lobster boat once. Worst three months of my life. Haven't touched one since."

"So you want me to eat one because you feel sorry for them? Or you want me to eat one because it'll be payback for the worst three months of your life?"

He grins at me. Nice smile too. "Both."

"Well, the next time I feel like wasting"—I look at the sign above them—"a whole lot of money, I'll keep it in mind. Or not." I turn my cart around, head toward the checkout.

I hear him laugh, which surprises me, but I don't bother to look back. Nice eyes, nice smile, but that hair? No way. Besides, guys just aren't worth the trouble.

5

Mom doesn't come home that night but she's back in the morning, lying on the sofa with her eyes closed when I come downstairs. There's a hickey on her neck. I pretend I don't see it.

"Hey, baby," she says. "Taxis around here suck. Also, I really need some coffee. Why didn't you buy any?"

"Because we don't have a coffeemaker."

"Oh." She's silent for a moment, then opens her eyes and gives me a big smile. "There's a fifty in my bag upstairs. Take it and go get yourself some breakfast, okay?"

"And coffee."

"And coffee," she says, still smiling. Even after being up all night she looks great. Makeup, perfect. Hair, perfect. I don't even want to think about what

I look like right now. I go get the money, then grab the car keys and head for the door.

There's a donut place down the road, and I buy Mom a jelly and a plain plus a large coffee. I buy a cream-filled donut for myself.

"Another coffee?" the woman working the counter asks.

I've never been able to drink coffee. It smells great but that's all it's got going for it.

"Can I get a soda?"

The woman laughs until she realizes I'm serious. After that I'm sent to a display case by the wall, and have to grab a soda while everyone watches me. Great job fitting in. I'm glad Mom isn't here to see this. Next time I'll order orange juice or something.

When I get back, Mom is still lying down, but she sits up as soon as I come in, coughing a little and eyeing the coffee like it's made of gold. I think the hickey has gotten even bigger while I've been gone.

"Here," I say, and pass her the coffee and donuts.

"What's going on with you?"

"Nothing."

She sighs. "It's just a hickey, baby. You shouldn't

be so uptight. You're young, have some fun once in a while."

"Mom."

"Oh, right," she says, and rolls her eyes at me. "I forgot how you are."

"Drink your coffee," I tell her, and nudge the donut bag with a finger. "I got you something to eat too."

"My favorites!" she says, and grins at me. We eat on the sofa and I listen while Mom talks about what she did last night. She liked the casino, tells me it was new-looking and very large. "So many people!" she says. "I had a great time."

"So how much money did you lose?" I ask, and she laughs, rolls her eyes at me.

"Oh, everything we had, of course."

Mom would never do that. She isn't Dad's biggest fan—he's the one person who ever really hurt her—but she will admit he taught her one useful thing: Don't waste money on things you can't win at/don't need. A lot of people like us do drugs or take expensive vacations or buy luxury cars. Conspicuous things.

We don't do that. We buy sensible cars, neutral-colored midsize sedans that blend in. We don't go anywhere expensive unless it's for a job—the rest of the time it's crappy apartments, hotels, or houses. And while Mom hasn't ever told me not to do drugs—she's just not like that—she's never had anything nice to say about people who do what we do and use. She says drugs make you sloppy, that they ruin what's best about what we do, the moment we're inside a place we shouldn't be and are holding things that aren't ours. She says there's no rush like it.

I've never felt it. I've never told her that. I don't want her to be disappointed in me.

"So . . ." I say, and point at her neck. "What did happen?"

It turns out she met an architect, a local guy who renovates houses. "And not just any houses," she says. "Our kind of houses. I spent a lot of time with him. He said the people around here, the rich ones down in Heaven, are pains in the asses."

I finish my donut and drink some soda. "What's his name?"

Mom looks blank for a second. "Richard? No, no. Robert. Nice guy. Very sweet. Good kisser." She laughs when I blush. "He told me a bunch of stories—gossip, mostly—but a few of them . . ."

"A few of them what?" I say, just like I'm supposed to, and Mom grins.

"Okay, get this. He said at the job he just finished, the people were so insistent on having a certain kind of molding put in that even though ripping the old molding out screwed up the security system, they didn't care. Plus, he has a brother—no, wait, a cousin—who does most of the alarm systems around here. The big companies use him as a contractor because it costs too much to have an entire office here. I saw his card . . ."

She leans over and fishes around in her purse, pulls out a wallet that isn't hers, and starts looking through it. "Here it is. It's a definite—"

"Is that his wallet?" I shouldn't be surprised but I am, a little. She does stuff like this all the time and I don't get it. She just said the guy was nice. Sweet, even. But she took his wallet. She didn't have to, didn't need to—but she did anyway.

"What?" she says, still distracted by the business card. "Oh baby, it was nothing. I flushed the credit cards before I left so he won't have to worry about some jerk getting them. All I got was stuff we need. People we might have to contact. Plus—" She shows me a fistful of bills. "Not too bad, right? And now we can go shopping, get a coffeemaker so you don't have to go out every morning. After all, I gotta look out for you, don't I?"

"Sure," I say, and watch Mom fold the bills away. The guy probably has a ton of money and, just like Mom said, it's not like we're going to use his credit cards. Plus I really don't want to have to go out and get coffee every morning. So it's really not that bad, all things considered. Right?

I never really even thought about stuff like this until I was thirteen and we robbed a rich old lady who lived in a huge house in upstate New York. We cleaned out all the silver she had, made enough to go to Manhattan and shop for two weeks. The day before we left the city, I was reading the paper and ran across an article about the robbery. The old lady wasn't as rich as we'd thought, had sold her house to pay back taxes her husband owed and gotten rid of her insurance policy on the silver because she couldn't afford it and was planning on selling the silver anyway.

I take a sip of soda. It's warm now, and leaves a bitter aftertaste in my mouth.

6

Mom tells me she's going out a little later, that she needs to find someone who knows more about Heaven. "There's a bar across the street from the town yacht club. I figure I'll go there, meet the bartender and maybe, if he's cute— well, if he is, he'd be a great source of information. And you, baby, should go to the beach. Not the public one. There's a little one in Heaven, remember? Go and get some sun, meet a few people, and find out what you can."

I nod, even though it's the last thing I feel like doing. Mom must know that because she doesn't leave till I'm in a cab and headed for the beach.

I'm not good with people like Mom is. She can start a conversation with anyone and—well, I can too, if I have to, but I don't like it. Whenever I talk to someone it's always the same; I'm nice, they talk, I remember anything important and then tell Mom. Jobs are the only time I talk to anyone besides her. If we live somewhere where we have neighbors, like in an apartment, we have to keep a low profile, be forgettable, and that means keeping to ourselves.

When I was younger I used to talk to kids I met in the library when I was doing research, but as I got older they were always there in groups and only talked to each other, discussing homework and complaining about curfews, things I knew nothing about.

When I get to the beach I decide I'll go in, lie out in the sun for a few hours, and then leave. Chances are good I'll hear something—people do love to talk—and that'll be enough to keep Mom happy.

Getting in isn't a problem. I've been to private beaches before and usually there's a towel flunky or someone who's on the lookout for people who don't belong. Luckily, they're almost always bribable, but there's no one like that here. There's just a beach and a bunch of people lying on the sand or splashing around in the water. No towel flunkies. Not even a lifeguard.

I pick a spot that's far enough out so I can see everyone but still leave in a hurry if I need to, and spread out my towel. After a few minutes of pretending to look around to see if there's anyone I know (really to see if there are any conversations going that I should wander by and listen to) I get up and head toward the water.

I'm not a big fan of the ocean. Everyone says it's blue, but it's not. It just looks like a lot of dirty dishwater. And this particular stretch of beach seems to be mostly rocks and large dead jellyfish. Fun. I wade into the surf a little, look around again. I can't get over how easy it was to get in here. Mom would love it. She says rich people—the really rich—are so stupid it's funny.

It is funny, I guess, but as I leave the water and lie back down on my towel, closing my eyes, I can't help but wish I were somewhere a little different. Somewhere . . . I don't know. Somewhere where I could just be at the beach and not have to be thinking about—

"Do I know you?" Guy's voice.

"No," I say flatly, without opening my eyes. The last thing I need is some rich jerk trying to pick me up. Even if he did make the (not very) big effort of walking all the way over here.

"Are you sure? Because you seem really familiar and—"

"Hey, did you move my sunscreen? I can't find it anywhere." Girl's voice, sounding slightly upset.

"I didn't move it. It's right where you left it, Allison. And if you don't mind, I'm trying to talk—"

I open my eyes. "Look," I say, because I am so not interested in whatever drama is going to happen, but then I stop talking because looking down at me is . . . well. Someone who is so good-looking he can't possibly be real. You know those ads where a shirtless guy stands around all brooding and mysterious, like some sort of angel come down to earth? That guy is here, and he's looking at me.

I'm stunned for about three seconds, which is how long it takes me to realize that he knows exactly how good-looking he is. I can see it in his eyes. They look just like Mom's.

"James, Janet's right over there, you know," Allison says. She looks a lot like James except her hair isn't quite as blond and her eyes are a lot more friendly. "Like, watching us. And you promised—"

"Fine." James smirks at me, then walks off. I watch

him head back to a blanket near the water, sit down, and pull a long-haired girl into his arms.

"I'm sorry about that," Allison says. "I didn't mean to butt in. But see, Janet, the girl over there with him, is kind of my friend. Well, she's visiting the people next door and we went to school together. Not that she ever talked to me or anything, but still, she's just hooked up with my brother and, like, I—"

"It's okay." I don't think I've ever met anyone who talks so much.

"Are you sure?"

I nod.

"I'm Allison."

"Sydney."

"Do you . . ." She bites her lip. "Would it be okay if I sat here for a while? Seeing my brother make out with someone is, uh—"

"Weird."

"Exactly," she says, and sits down next to me.

Five minutes later we're heading down to where her brother and Janet are sitting because she has to get her wallet before we get ice cream. I think that's what we're doing, anyway. I'm not totally sure. She really does talk a lot.

"I'll just be a second," she says as she's digging through a huge bag. "I have all this stuff in here because I thought—"

"You thought you might see Brad," James says, and there's an edge of something unpleasant in his voice.

"Shut up." She laughs. "Brad is this guy I know," she tells me. "We met ages ago—his family and mine have been coming here forever. We're—"

"Friends," James says, with a grin in my direction. "Which is why you spent two hours getting ready to come to the beach this morning. Because it's important to look good for your friends, right, Ally?"

"I'd like to see you try to find totally waterproof makeup and then put it on so it looks natural, you loser." They tease each other for a couple of minutes—not in a mean way or anything, just teasing like—well, like I guess some families do—and I watch them, fascinated. I always wanted a brother or sister, someone to talk to about everything I can't say to Mom. Janet isn't interested at all, just yawns and glares at a girl who is looking at James.

"Okay, going," Allison says, leaning down and poking James's arm. "You want me to bring you back a soda or anything?"

James shakes his head and leans over, wraps one hand around my ankle. "Are you coming back with her?"

If I was younger or stupider—or both—I'd be a pile of mush right about now. But I know how much guys can be trusted, and that's not at all. So I just say, "Are you ready to go?" to Allison and pull away from him. He acts like nothing has happened, turns back to Janet. If she was smart she'd smack him, but she doesn't, just stares at him with her heart in her eyes. I almost feel sorry for her.

"Ready," Allison says, standing up and holding a wallet that probably cost as much as our car. I sigh. I'll get ice cream, I'll get some information, and then I'm out of here.

I don't get any information.

Well, I get some, but not the kind I'm supposed to. I learn that Allison can talk and eat ice cream at the same time. I learn she's going to college in the fall and is really excited about it. When she asks where I go to school, she listens and then asks questions that I have to make up answers to on the spot. The few times before I've mentioned that yeah, I'm in college, no one has cared what it's like. They just wanted to know where I was going.

I learn that Allison has a huge crush on Brad but that his family isn't rich like hers. She doesn't say it, but it becomes obvious as she talks about him.

"Mom hates that I keep inviting him over to the house every year because his dad, like, sells insurance, but oh, if you could see him. He's so cute! And he's not like the guys around here who are such losers. It's like, how many times can I listen to the same stupid stories about how everyone went to Amsterdam over winter break and got high? Whatever, you know?"

I nod and she keeps talking. Normally I'd write her off as a babbling idiot and make an excuse to leave, but she's not an idiot. She's nice. The only thing is, she keeps asking me about myself and then actually listens to the answers. I'm not used to that. In fact, most people just want to talk about themselves.

But Allison wants to know if I was nervous when I went away to college and what classes do I like best and do I need an extra napkin for my ice cream cone because she can just run right over and get me one.

I can't figure out what kind of game she's playing

and then, as she's pointing out the shoes some girl is wearing and asking what I think of them, I realize this is probably how normal people talk. How maybe people who could be friends talk. Weird. And kind of nice, too. But still weird.

"So where are you staying?" I ask, ready for the conversation to be one I'm familiar with. She tells me her family is in Heaven, in a house looking out over the ocean.

"Mom insists on calling it 'the cottage,' which is so stupid. I mean, are the words 'beach house' so bad? We're at the beach, for heaven's sake. Where are you staying?"

"What?" She wasn't supposed to ask that. I was supposed to say "Wow, your house sounds great," and then she was supposed to talk about it some more.

"Around here?"

I nod, hope she won't ask for anything more specific.

"For the whole summer?"

"I think so. You?"

"Oh, of course. Every year for as long as I can remember. Here until my parents' anniversary, which they celebrate by having a big party. Last year

I wanted to invite Brad but James said it might be weird for him. This year I'm going to invite him, though. I mean, you don't think it would be weird for him, right? It's not like we all run around naked or anything. Although I wouldn't mind . . ." She trails off and grins at me. "He's just—you know how some guys are, right?"

"Sure." I don't, but it doesn't matter. I should ask her about the party now.

I don't. Instead I point out a horrible tie-dyed jumper some unsuspecting infant has been forced to wear and we agree that tie-dye, along with all jewelry made from shells, should be outlawed. We sit and eat our ice cream and by the time I'm done, I've promised to come back to the beach and see her tomorrow.

"Thank God," she says. "It'll be so nice to hang out with someone who doesn't have their head up their ass."

"Thanks. I think."

She laughs. "Seriously, you're the first cool person I've met here in ages. Plus"—she clears her throat—"I'm pretty sure James will be happy to see you again."

I shrug. She gives me a look. "You don't like him?"

"He seems really . . . nice."

She's silent for a minute and then she says, "Everyone's crazy about him. You know how in some families there's one person everyone wants you to be like? Like, they're perfect and what you're supposed to be?"

"I know exactly what you mean," I tell her. And I do.

he next morning Mom says she has something for me to do. I rub my face with both hands and stare at her sleepily. She's caught a cold or something, was up most of the night coughing.

"You should go see a doctor," I tell her as I'm fixing her coffee and she's looking at a map, marking off houses with little red Xs.

She nods, which I know means she isn't even listening. I sigh, put her coffee in front of her, and then fix myself some cereal.

"So what do you want me to do?"

"Baby, can't you eat something with marshmallows or frosting on it like a normal kid?"

I sigh again. The map thing must not be going as well as she wants it to. "I had a donut yesterday."

"Only old people eat those wheat biscuit things."

"I like them."

She finishes marking Xs on her map and drops her pen on the table. "Well, at least that's finally done. Did you meet anyone at the beach?"

"Not really."

She gives me a look and I take an extra big bite of cereal just to be obnoxious, crunching it loudly between my teeth.

"I didn't send you there to work on your tan," she says, but she's grinning now. Teasing. Mostly.

"So do you finally feel like telling me what it is you want me to do?" I take another big bite of cereal.

"Smartass." She grins. "I need you to see what you can dig up on the Donaldson house." She points at an X on the map.

"What do you have?"

She tells me what she's learned, which is that the house was built in the early twentieth century, that it's survived a bunch of hurricanes, and that the family that owns it comes to stay every summer.

"Wow, I bet that doesn't describe any other house in Heaven."

She raises an eyebrow at me. "Danielle."

"Sorry." I wash out my bowl and put it away, re-fill her coffee. She's looking at the map again, and I watch her trace her finger across streets, tracking ways to leave town.

"So what are you doing today?" I ask.

"Don't know yet."

Uh huh. Bartender again, I bet. "What's his name?"

"Christ, you sound like someone's whiny mother. Glenn, okay?"

"Glenn what?"

She smirks. "We haven't got around to exchanging last names yet."

I feel my face flush, and her smirk gets wider. She knows I don't like it when she talks like this. "Well, tell him thanks a lot for giving you a cold, will you?"

"We need an in to the Donaldson place," she says, looking back down at the map. "Quit standing around here all prune-faced because I like to have fun and go get some information we can use."

"Mom," I say, hurt, but she keeps looking at the map. I wait a moment, but she still doesn't look at me, and so I head upstairs.

I was fifteen the first and only time I had sex. The

guy's name was Roger, he was twenty, and he and Mom had hooked up. He was a waiter at some resort she was checking out, and she fell for him as much as she ever does anyone, which isn't much at all. They were together about three weeks.

He was hot and funny and I had a huge crush on him, which I thought I'd kept a secret. Looking back, I suppose I couldn't have been more obvious. I would drop whatever I was doing when he came over and hang around until Mom took him back to her room. Sometimes when they were done he'd watch television with me till he had to leave.

And then one night he slept over and came into the kitchen when I was making breakfast the next morning. I can still remember hearing him come up behind me, how I held my breath and just waited. Hoped.

I suppose since he was so much older I should say he took advantage of me or something, but the truth is I wanted him so bad even my teeth hurt with it and the sex was amazing. I know first times aren't supposed to be great, but Roger had plenty of practice.

What wasn't amazing was waking up alone afterward and hearing him and Mom talking in the hall.

"Did you just do what I think you did?"

"Wait, you're mad? The other day you said you could tell I thought she was hot."

Mom laughed. "You're a piece of work."

"Hey, you said you wanted the best for her. What was I supposed to think?"

"You treat her right?"

"Absolutely. You know how I am."

"Yeah, a jackass," Mom said, but her voice was light, like it always was when she talked to guys, and I heard them kiss. He'd just fucked me and then gone and kissed her. He was okay with it. She was okay with it. The only one who wasn't okay with it was me.

After he left, I told her I wanted to leave. I actually think I said that we had to leave. She stared at me for a long time but finally said, "Okay."

In the car, on our way out of town, she said, "You know, what happened earlier, it's not something to worry about. I'm not upset. He's a good-looking guy and it's perfectly natural that you'd—"

"Stop," I said, so angry I was shaking. "Don't say . . . don't say another word." I'd never spoken to her like that before. I've never spoken to her like that since. But I did then, and she listened. She's never mentioned it again.

I get dressed and, at the last second, throw my swimsuit in my bag. Just in case, I tell myself. I won't need it, but it's good to be prepared. When I go back downstairs Mom's painting her toenails and looking perfectly happy, like she didn't just dismiss me before. Like she doesn't know why I'm so uncomfortable discussing her "love life." I grab the car keys and head for the door feeling hurt and angry. Mostly hurt.

"Baby—"

"What?" I'm trying to sound furious but my voice comes out watery, faint.

She gets up and walks over to me, moving pigeon-toed so she won't smudge her toenails. It makes me smile in spite of myself. She sees my grin and gives me one in return, wraps her arms around me.

"You know I can't do this without you, right?" she whispers.

I nod, wondering if that's true, but for now, just glad to hear her say it, and then rest my head on her shoulder. I'm taller than she is, but she's always going to be a million times bigger than I'll ever be.

When I get to the records office I can tell they'd definitely have something on the Donaldson house, but the man working behind the counter has the obsessive look of someone who remembers anyone who's ever asked him a question. That won't do at all and so I head back to the car.

What I'm doing now is what I like best about what we do. It's actually the only thing. Mom loves sliding into someone's house and making what they own hers, but I like finding out when a house was built or how much the real estate taxes were in 1922. I guess it's because I never went to school. We've never stayed in one place for long, and the very few times anyone asked, Mom just said she taught me at home.

And really, I guess, she sort of has. Mom says I haven't missed anything by not going to school, that I know how to read and write and figure out our percentage from a sale to our fence and "that's more than most people know, baby. Some kids go to school and leave not knowing how to write their own name. You can do that and you can tell plate from sterling just by looking at it. That's education." I guess she's right, but sometimes I wonder what it would have been like to go, to have to rush down hallways between classes, to have homework, to take tests.

Well, not the test part, though I did wonder about the SATs for a while and even bought a practice book and took one of the tests just to see what it felt like. It didn't feel like much of anything but I suppose that's because I know I'll never do something like go to college.

I head to the library next but it's got lots of copies of the latest bestsellers and not much else. Now I'll have to try historical societies. I sign up to use one of the library's computers and when I leave, I have the names and addresses of five historical societies to visit, all local. I can't imagine the entire state has enough stuff to fill up five places, but I guess people around here like their history.

My first stop is just outside West Hill. A plaque on the door says the Wearing Society is run by volunteers and so I stand outside for a minute, preparing for stories about grandchildren, cats, and cruises. But when I go in, the woman working at the visitor's desk cuts me off in the middle of my carefully worded ramble (it's better if you sound unsure—acting like you know exactly what you're looking for is memorable, especially if what you ask about turns up robbed a little later) by saying, "Yes, yes. You want the Donaldson house. We have something in the reading room."

So I head into the reading room.

8

The reading room is about the size of a closet, and the woman working there takes a break from a complicated knitting project and rummages around in a box for a while before handing me a small pamphlet.

"We're getting bookcases next month," she says. "Donated by the . . ."

I tune her out and nod politely, hope that whatever she's given me to read is going to be worth the story (which seems to be about salt ponds) I'm stuck listening to.

It is.

It's not a very long pamphlet, about fifteen pages, and the author spends three pages talking about how he's related to the Donaldsons through the marriage of a cousin a hundred years ago, and how that led to his interest in the Donaldson house, which "yielded gracious permission to visit the estate." I grit my teeth—I hate how boring and full of suck-up crap these things are—and turn the page.

I was hoping for a description I could use to create a basic layout, but instead I get photos. Lots and lots of photos, pictures of what seems to be every room of the house. There's even a floor plan with notes. I skim them to see if there are any security references. There are, and the author has even named the company that set up the current system. Mom's going to be overjoyed.

I force myself to wait ten more minutes and then get up, pick up a copy of some book they've got for sale. I ask if I can buy it, then hold up the pamphlet and add, "And a copy of this too, if you have one."

I can buy the book, which the knitting lady tells me was written by her brother, but the Donaldson pamphlet isn't for sale.

"I could make you a copy though," she says. "But we'd have to charge you ten cents a page."

"Well," I say, trying to look thoughtful and not really happy, "I guess that would be okay."

I leave forty-five minutes later, $43.50 poorer—

that stupid book was $42—and my head full of stories about the reading room lady's family. It seems their claim to fame is participating in some Indian massacre that took place three hundred years ago. I wouldn't be proud of that, but she sure seems to be.

In the car, I tuck the photocopied pages into the book and slide it under the seat. I can't wait to show it to Mom. She'll be so happy. I pull out of the parking lot and onto the road, humming under my breath.

Five minutes later I realize I've driven toward the beach, to Heaven. There's no point in going. I've got everything Mom and I need. I don't need to go to the beach now, especially not to hang out with someone. I should turn the car around and head back to the house.

I keep driving. I change into my bathing suit in the lobby bathroom in Heaven's inn, mixing with the tourists who've come to gawk and talk about their sunburns, and then go to the beach. When I get there I stand outside, on the sidewalk, hesitating. It was stupid to come, won't help with what we're here for. I should just go.

"Sydney!"

Allison is waving at me. I stand there for a

second, still unsure, then wave back and head onto the beach.

"There you are!" she says when I reach her. "I thought maybe you weren't coming."

"I meant to be here earlier, but you know how it is." Because I'm sure she spends lots of time being bored off her ass reading up on old houses she and her mom plan to rob.

"Parents?" she says, making a face.

Okay, sure, why not? "Yeah." I mean, it is sort of true.

"Well, sit down. Larry Harrison just made his yearly appearance and I need help coping."

"Why? Is he hot?"

She grins. "If you like seventy-year-old men who wear Speedos."

I laugh and sit down next to her. "Sounds hot."

"I think even the ocean screamed. So what's going on with your parents?"

"What? Oh, the usual. Blah blah do this, blah blah do that."

"What do they want you to do?"

"You know, parent-type stuff." I'm not used to people actually being interested in what's going on with me, and quickly change the subject to something safer. "How are things with that guy? Brad, right?"

She grins at me. "I saw him! Last night I went into town with the housekeeper and saw him at the grocery store. I asked him if he would meet me here today and I could tell he was going to say yes but then he didn't. You know what I mean, right? Sometimes guys say something, but you know they want to say something else."

"I thought they just lied all the time."

She laughs and I shift a little, uncomfortable with the conversation. With what I've just said. I don't talk about how I feel about guys—I don't ever talk about anything real with anyone.

"Anyway, James can be overprotective and I think he might have said something to Brad the last time we saw him. It's so stupid. I mean, it's not like I'm going to marry the guy or anything. I just—a lot of people around here are . . ."

She makes a face. "It's like they look down on everyone. I hate that. Plus"—she grins at me—"Brad is so adorable. I just have to figure out a way to—I know! Okay, what do you think of this? I get up tomorrow morning and go running or something, end up by his house—his family rents the same place every year, down by the big pond—do you know the one I'm talking about? And then I can see him and—"

"For that plan to work, people would have to actually believe you exercise, Ally." James has shown up, stands grinning down at us. "Hey again," he tells me. "I'm glad you—"

"Did you say something to Brad?" Allison says, cutting him off.

"I wouldn't do that." James sounds upset. "I know you like him. But really, how well do you know him? I mean, hanging out once in a while in the summer when we were kids . . . it's different now that we're older."

"You say," Allison says sharply, and then rolls over onto her stomach and closes her eyes.

James sighs. "Fine." He looks at me, smiles, and holds out one hand. "Want to go for a walk, give Ally a chance to sulk in—well, semiprivate?"

"I don't really feel like a walk." I try to sound polite, but know I fail.

He tilts his head a little to the side. "You mean you don't really feel like a walk with me."

"That's right."

His face falls and he drops his hand, then turns and walks off down the beach. I admit, he's hot and has the whole slumped-shoulders-oh-you've-hurt-me thing down pretty well. But I also see he's checking out girls who are walking by, smiling the way he was just smiling at me. He could use lessons from Mom. The thought makes me laugh in a strange, tight-throated way, and I look over at Allison, who is still lying on her stomach. Her eyes are open though, and she's looking at me, a little frown on her face.

"What?" I say.

She props herself up on her elbows and looks over at James, still walking along the beach, and then back at me. "James is . . . he knows he's James Donaldson, you know? My dad says that—"

She keeps talking but I can't hear her. All I hear is one word.

Donaldson.

9

Mom is home when I get there, lying on the sofa again. She sits up as soon as I walk in though, and before I've even opened my mouth I can tell she knows I've found something because a huge smile breaks across her face.

"Tell me, baby," she says. "Tell me everything."

So I do. Except I don't tell her about the beach, about how I was just there and left in a hurry, saying I had to go and making up some lame excuse. I don't tell her who I was with. I just tell her about the pamphlet.

"It's perfect," she says after she's looked through the copy, and throws her arms around me. "You did good today. You did so good."

I pull back and look at her. Her eyes are shining and I can tell she's already planning.

"So what's next?"

"You'll see, baby," she says. "In the meantime, we're going to have to celebrate tonight. How does a lobster dinner sound?"

"Sounds good. Where are we going?"

It turns out we aren't going anywhere because apparently I'm going to the grocery store to get lobsters.

"Low profile now, baby," Mom says. "We gotta start getting ready." I want to ask if that applies to the bartender, but Mom is happy and I don't want to spoil that.

The grocery store is packed. I can't find a space in the lot and end up parking by some town office across the street, have to back up and then pull into the spot again because the lines are so narrow. As I get out of the car I realize someone's standing by my back bumper. Great. A lecture about driving from a cranky old person, or better yet, it'll be someone who wants me to sign a petition against a traffic light or . . . wait a minute. I'd recognize that hair anywhere. It's the guy from the other day.

"What are you doing by my car?"

"Hey there," he says. His smile really is nice, though up close I can see his bottom teeth are just a little crooked. Somehow that looks okay on him though, sort of like the hair. I never think guys are cute, but he really kind of is. Which makes me feel strange.

"Yeah, whatever. Again, what are you doing by my car?"

He points at a sign above the parking space. It says EMPLOYEES ONLY.

"So? I'm pretty sure there aren't any employees here, what with the parking lot being empty and all." I start to walk toward the store.

"You shouldn't leave your car here."

"I don't think any fights are going to break out over the parking space."

"I'm just saying that if you don't move your car, you might get a ticket."

"Thanks for the tip."

"Seriously," he says, and he's caught up to me, is standing next to me as I wait to cross the street. I look over at him. His hair really is weird. Not just the cut, but the color too. I thought it was brown, but now that he's right next to me I can see there's bits of dark blond and even red in there. I think I could look at him all day and worse, I want to keep talking to him. This has to stop.

"Okay," I say. "Seriously thank you very much for letting me know. Bye."

"You're new to town, right?"

Finally, no traffic. I start to cross the street.

"I'll take that as a yes. Are you here for the summer?"

"Maybe."

"Maybe yes? Maybe no?"

"What are you, a cop?"

No reply, and when I look over he's grinning at me. Oh shit. A cop.

"Don't look so freaked out," he says.

Okay, damage control and then I've got to get away from him. "I don't look freaked out."

"Yeah, you do."

"No, I don't. And I'll go move my car, all right?"

"You don't have to do that. No one's at work in that office past three anyway."

"So you're just giving me a hard time."

"No, I was just pointing out a sign."

"And now you're what, following me?"

He laughs. "Wow, paranoid too. I'm going to the

grocery store and was cutting through the lot when I saw you."

"And talked to me."

"True. If it makes you feel better though, I also talked to Mr. Martin on my way here. He was waiting for his daughter to pick him up."

"Great. Bye." Finally, I've reached the damn store. I grab a basket and move toward the back, hoping he doesn't follow me. It just figures that he's a cop. It really does.

The seafood counter is crowded, but the cop appears to be done talking to me. Good. Really, it is. If only he wasn't so cute. I wait while someone buys cod and someone else buys scallops and then someone complains about crabmeat. I don't look around to see if a certain Mr. Strange Hair is nearby. When it's finally my turn I order the lobsters and am told I have to wait while they're steamed.

"Fine," I say, pasting a smile on my face, and wander around the frozen fish section. At least this way by the time I'm done the cop will be gone. I can't believe this. I wish we'd never come to Heaven.

The seafood counter lady calls me over and hands me the lobsters, all wrapped up and ready to go. I wait in line to pay and pick up a couple of magazines for Mom—she likes presents—and then head back to the car.

The cop is there, sitting on my car with three bags of groceries around him.

"Get off my—" No. No. Wrong. I can't let him know I'm mad because he's cute. And a cop. Be polite, get gone. Low profile.

"Is there a reason you're sitting on my car?" Better. Nice. Polite.

"Got lobsters, huh?"

"Yes. And I really need to . . . uh . . . get them home." Even though they're already dead. And cooked. Maybe he hasn't noticed.

"So, you live around here?" I think he's noticed.

"If I say yes, will you get off my car?"

"Is that a yes?"

"What do you think?"

He grins at me and gets off the car. That was easier than I thought.

"I'm Greg. And you are?"

"Leaving." I unlock my door. "Can you move your bags?"

"Sure." He picks one up. "Anyway, like I was saying,

I'm Greg. I work—" He points at the police station.

"Yeah, I think I figured that one out already."

He grins at me again and picks up the other bags. "So where did you go to high school?"

I ignore him.

"I went to North Stonington. Graduated two years ago and then went to the academy."

"Right out of high school? Why?" I ask before I can help myself. I mean, I know cops have to become cops, but I always figured they did it after they failed at selling shoes or something.

"I don't know. I guess because my dad was a cop."

Oh goody, a law enforcement family. This just keeps getting better and better. His father is probably the sheriff or something.

"So you're telling me you and your family are cops and I'd better, what? Watch my step? Stay on the straight and narrow?"

"'Stay on the straight and narrow'? I've never heard anyone say that before. Other than on television, I mean. Anyway, I suppose I could put out a bulletin on you if you wanted. But then I don't have a name to give."

"Gee, too bad."

"You're not going to tell me your name?"

"That's right," I say, and open my car door. "But if there's anything else you want to tell me, you just go ahead and keep talking. When I drive away, I'll still be listening, I promise."

"What do you want to know?"

"Oh, where to start? Blood type? Birth sign?"

He holds the door open for me as I slide inside, causing my insides to go all fluttery, and drops one of his bags. I hear the distinct sound of glass breaking.

"Very smooth," I say, and my voice actually sounds a little fluttery too.

"Hey, at least I'm trying here. Also, AB and Gemini."

"I was kidding. Now if you don't mind—"

"Okay," he says, and steps away from the car. "You have got to be a Cancer. Please notice that I'm not making any crab jokes."

"Except that you just sort of made one, didn't you?" I shut the door, start the car. He knocks on the window. I ignore him.

He knocks again. I put the car in reverse.

"See you around, Hortense," he says.

I stop. I roll down the window. "Hortense?" My

God, that's worse than Helen.

"Well, since you won't tell me your name, I have to call you something."

"And that's the best you could come up with?"

"For now. Maybe when I see you again—"

I roll up the window, start to drive away. I can see him in the rearview mirror. He's gathering up his groceries. I didn't realize so much stuff fell out of that one bag. I sigh, stop the car, and get out. I gather up two cans of green beans, a package of hamburger, and two boxes of macaroni and cheese and take them over to him.

"Here."

He looks up at me. "Thanks." He sounds a little surprised. His eyes are really very green.

"Whatever. I just didn't want to run over groceries. Even if they are yours."

"I'll say one thing for you. You're a hell of a sweet talker."

"Bye." I head back to the car.

"See you around, Hortense."

"Not likely."

I look in the rearview mirror again as I drive away. He's walking across the parking lot. It looks like he's whistling. What a weird guy. Even for a cop, he's weird. So weird, it totally overrides the fact that he's cute. And the fact that he's the first guy I've wanted to talk to for years.

"Also," I say, squinting at my face in the mirror, "there is no way I look like a Hortense."

10

Mom goes out after we eat our lobsters and as soon as she gets in the next morning, she tells me there's a party at the yacht club tonight and that we're going. The bartender, Glenn, told her about it. She tells me this in an offhand way, which means that not only is this party important, she's done with Glenn. Which also means that now there's someone else.

I wait, and sure enough the conversation switches to Harold. He's the real estate agent she told me about before, the one the first agent, Sharon, didn't like.

Harold specializes in beachfront property, and although I'm sure he doesn't know this yet, he'll be totally in love with Mom in about a day. I listen to her talk about what kind of houses she thinks Harold could get us, what she's going to say when she meets him, and then we talk about what needs to happen tonight.

Mom is going to the party as "Miranda." Miranda is staying with her friend Tom ("He's in banking, darling, you've heard of him, right?") for a few days at Tom's friend's house. Tom can't come to the party ("Big deal, couldn't be helped, you know how it is") but he's told her to go and enjoy herself.

My story is even simpler. I don't have one. People my age are dragged to these things, stand around drinking, and then head off to get high and/or plot ways to escape. The only thing I'll be asked is if I have anything or know someone who does. You'd think I'd end up coming away from these things with more information than Mom but I never do. She just has a knack for working people, one I'm not sure I'll ever have.

I take her to Heaven after eight and drop her off. Then I drive around for an hour, killing time, and park by a restaurant next to the yacht club. Five minutes later I'm at the party, sliding right past the stressed-out-looking party planner, who is clearly up to her eyeballs in some sort of catering crisis. There are always catering crises at these things.

I see Mom right away. She loves dressing up and

she looks gorgeous tonight, wearing a white dress with her hair down, a tumble of curls cascading over her shoulders. She's standing so a nearby light shines on her just right, making her skin glow. She's talking to a red-faced guy in a blue blazer who is clearly thrilled to have someone like Mom talking to him. She looks like she's having fun. She probably is, though not in the way the red-faced guy thinks.

I grab a drink at the bar, where the bartender is so busy he doesn't even have time to pretend he wants to see proof I'm twenty-one, and then walk around the room slowly, listening to conversations. They're all very boring, but I find out that someone named Sandy has just bought a yacht and that the Donaldsons should be sending out invitations to their party soon. Mom will be happy to know that. I go back to the bar and get myself another drink and walk around the room again. I'm asked if I know where someone named Red is by a very stoned girl and her equally stoned date. I hear about Sandy and his yacht another two times.

After I get asked if I want something to "help me relax" by a guy who puts his hand on my ass, I hit the bar again and then head outside, feeling a little dizzy from all the people walking around (and okay, the drinks). There's a wooden walkway that looks out over the water with little paths that lead down to the yachts. I can see their shadows on the water from where I'm standing.

"Peaceful, isn't it?"

I turn, see James has come up behind me.

"Relax," he says, holding up his hands. "I just came out for some air. Didn't know you were here till just now, I swear."

I look away from him, stare back out into the dark.

"Okay," he says. "The truth is, I thought you looked lonely. And I—these things always make me feel that way too."

"Really?" I shouldn't believe him—I know better, I so know better—but I am lonely. Parties like this always make it worse, remind me that I've never been to one for fun, that I've never been to a party as me. I've always played someone else, always had a job to do.

"Yeah," he says, moving closer, and I can tell he's going to try and kiss me.

I could let him. No one can fool you like you can

fool yourself—Mom says that all the time—but it's just one kiss, a kiss from a great-looking guy. Just a connection, no matter how brief, with someone. I close my eyes.

"Sydney?"

I turn around and Allison is walking toward us, smiling.

"I thought that was you. I love your dress! I've been looking all over for a blue dress, but they're always the wrong shade of blue, you know? Too light or too dark or—you know what? Come with me to get a drink and tell me where you got it, okay?" She loops her arm through mine. "James, do you want anything?"

"Sure, I'll have a drink," he says easily, but gives Allison a look when we start to walk off, one I can't read. She raises her eyebrows at him. He shakes his head, says, "You know, in case you forgot, I have a mother already."

"Oh, so funny," Allison says. "She's looking for you, by the way. There's someone else she wants you to meet."

"Did you get a name?"

"Wasn't introduced," she says, her voice shading

sad for a moment, and then turns back toward me. "Oh! Your shoes! I have a pair just like them. Don't you just love them? Did you know they make them in yellow? I almost bought a pair but then I realized I wasn't sure what would go with them—"

She keeps talking as we walk to the bar. It's so crowded I wait off to one side while she goes and orders drinks. I wonder what's going on. The whole thing with her and James was a little weird.

"Weren't you going to get James something?" I ask when she comes back with only two glasses.

"I would if he hadn't wandered off," Allison says cheerfully, and hands me a drink. I take a sip. It's club soda. I look at her.

"I saw you go outside when I was trapped talking to my cousin Blair." Allison makes a face. "She's so boring! Anyway, you were wobbling a little and I'm not one of those 'drinking is bad!' people, but, like, some guys around here are kind of jerks, so . . ."

She takes a sip of her drink. "Besides, puking during one of these things? It's awful. Everyone can hear you. Now, I'm totally dying to know where you got your dress. You have to tell me!"

"What's going on with you and James?"

"Oh, nothing. He's just . . . he couldn't believe you didn't go walking with him on the beach and when he doesn't get his way he can be—oh crap. There's Blair." She moves so she's standing behind me. "I can't handle another conversation about her stupid trip to the Bahamas where she—" She breaks off as someone bumps into her.

"I'm so sorry," a voice says. A voice I know. "I didn't even see anyone there . . . oh, hi, Allison. Are you okay?"

"I'm fine," Allison says, laughing. "Last year I got an elbow in the ribs from someone desperate to get to the bar before it closed. Miranda, right?"

"That's right."

"Sydney, this is—"

I turn and look at my mother standing in front of me. There is a polite smile on her face, the smile of someone meeting a stranger, and it doesn't waver at all as she says it's nice to meet me.

"You too," I say, and watch her turn all her attention on Allison, making her shine under her gaze.

"I'm actually glad I bumped into you," Mom tells her. "I was trying to escape from a dreadful conversation about security bonds or something—honestly, just because I'm with a banker, it doesn't mean I know anything about banking. Actually, I'd love to hear the rest of the story you started before. How on earth did your mother manage to find replacement flowers for that party on such short notice?"

"Do you want to get another drink?" I ask Allison. I know I shouldn't be saying this, that I should leave Allison with Mom and go, but I just—I don't like what Mom is doing. Allison's nice, the kind of nice that Mom takes advantage of, and it's bothering me more than usual.

Mom gives me the faintest and fastest of looks, annoyance flickering through her gaze even as her smile stays glittering on her face.

"Never mind," I say, and when Mom's gaze flickers over me again, add, "I'll be right back," leaving to let her work Allison. I hope Allison will decide to come with me, but she doesn't, and is still talking to Mom when I'm waiting at the bar again.

Not my problem, I tell myself. Allison talking is what we want. The bartender tells me all that's left is scotch. I take the glass I'm given and sip it slowly, trying not to make a face.

"They must be down to scotch."

James again. I put my glass on the bar.

"How did you guess?"

"It always happens. In about ten minutes there'll be a run on the bar, and then everyone will go home."

"So I guess you're leaving?"

"I was going to, but then I saw you and realized I hadn't said good-bye."

"Right."

He grins at me. "You don't like me, do you?"

"I don't know you."

"Well, we could change that," he says, and draws me toward the side of the room, into a corner the caterers were using earlier. It's just the two of us now, the last of the catering crew heading down a hall beside us.

"I'd really like to get to know you," he tells me, and cups my jaw with one hand, tilting my face up toward his. Very smooth. Too smooth. I lift my foot up, ready to mash it down on top of his, and then someone says, "Look, I get that you have to pack up. I'm just asking if it's necessary for you to pack up by leaving three vans in the middle of the street. Could you maybe just pull them over to the side—oh, sorry about that."

Whoever's talking bumps into me and I stumble. James's arms—naturally—catch and close tight around me.

"Are you okay? I didn't mean to—oh. Hey."

I turn around to see who's talking to me. It's Greg the cop. He's in his uniform tonight. He actually looks kind of cute—No! Not going there. Dark blue polyester does nothing for anyone. Not even him.

"I'm fine," I say.

He nods, glances at James's arms around me.

"Sorry about all that," he says to James. "Are you okay?" James doesn't reply, just stares at me like I'm the only person in the world. I barely manage not to roll my eyes.

"Okay then," Greg says, "guess you'll live." He looks back at me, and I wonder if he's going to bring up the grocery store or worse, call me Hortense, but then one of the catering people calls out, "Look, we're moving the vans, all right? There's no need to have a tow truck come down here," and he turns away.

"Hey man, I didn't call anyone," he says. "Someone else must have complained. How much stuff do you have left? Just this and this? Okay, you get that and

I'll get this—damn, what's in here, bricks?"

He's still talking as he leaves the hallway and heads outside. He turns back once and I look away quickly, focus on James.

James is still giving me that stupid look. I can't believe I ever thought, even for a second, about letting him kiss me. There's no way this guy would ever make me feel less alone. I slide out of his arms, walk away without looking back.

Mom is already in the car when I get there, sitting in the driver's seat with her eyes closed and her hands resting lightly on the steering wheel.

"Didn't think you'd beat me here," I say.

"The Donaldson girl wore me out. Talks a mile a minute, I swear. 'I love this, I love that, oh my God, I just love—'"

"She's not like that. I mean, she didn't seem like that to me. She seemed nice."

Mom snorts. "Of course she's like that. Trust me, baby, if you were some tourist she passed on the street she'd be a lot less 'nice.'"

"I guess," I say, and think of Allison complaining about how the people she's expected to hang out

80

with are awful and shallow. I remember how much she likes Brad, a regular guy, a guy who doesn't even have connections to money. Mom would call Brad— she wouldn't call him anything. He'd have nothing she could use, and so she'd never notice him.

"So," Mom says, interrupting my thoughts. "Who were you with over in the corner? I saw you as I was leaving. Next time try a closet. They're more private and a lot more fun." She winks at me.

"What?" She thought I was with James? That I'd want to be with someone like him? Someone like— well, someone like us?

"Hey, it's about time you started to live a little. Maybe now you won't get all uptight whenever I'm having fun. That'd be nice."

"Mom—" I say, stung.

"Look, I could be really pissed that you talked to the Donaldson girl and didn't get anything and then almost blew it when I came over to take care of things. But I'm not. So why don't you—" She coughs, loud and harsh. I watch her as she tries to stop, pressing her lips together, but the coughs keep coming, making her shudder and hunch forward.

I lean over and rub her back. She rolls her eyes

at me but doesn't move away. I can feel her back shuddering under my hand, the coughs shaking her whole body.

"Mom?"

She shakes her head, coughs once more, and then sits up, starts the car.

"Are you okay?" I ask.

"Fine, baby. Don't I look it?"

"Of course," I say automatically. "It's just . . . you look kind of tired." She does, which frightens me. I've seen Mom look angry, happy, focused. But never tired. Not like this, a weary expression on her face, creating lines around her eyes and mouth. I've never thought of Mom as old, ever, but right now she looks like she is.

"Oh, it was just that crap champagne," she says, and closes her eyes briefly. I look at the road flying by and press my hands against the seat. This is the Mom I know, the one who is daring in ways I will never be. I would never drive blind down a road, not ever.

When she opens her eyes she turns, smiles at me. She looks like herself again. "You okay?"

"I'm fine."

"How many times have we done this, baby?"

"A lot."

"And we always get it done, don't we?"

"Yeah," I say. "We do."

11

Mom wakes me up at seven and tells me she wants donuts.

"That's great," I say. "Bring me back one." I pull a pillow over my head and shut my eyes.

"Okay," Mom sighs. "I'll just put away all the stuff I was working on and drive to the store. I didn't realize you were busy."

Now it's my turn to sigh. "I'm trying to sleep."

"Please, baby," Mom says, sitting down next to me. "I have to meet Harold later and—"

"Fine," I say, because I know where this is going and that's Mom staying here until I agree. "But you know, in the time it took you to wake me up you'd have been halfway there already."

"But I don't want to go. And besides, what good is being halfway there?" She kisses my forehead and goes back downstairs, humming. I get up and throw on some clothes, head out to the car.

The donut place is packed and I'm stuck waiting in line behind a guy with two screaming children who seem determined to try and shatter the windows. Mom always wants donuts or some sort of pastry after a good night. I once had to drive to four convenience stores in middle-of-nowhere Maryland to find something for her to eat after we'd hit a place way out on the Eastern Shore.

The screaming children are really going at it now, both of them shrieking "You touched me!" at the same time. I close my eyes and rub my forehead.

"Hey, Hortense. I was just thinking about you."

I turn around and see Greg standing behind me. He's not in uniform today. He has a bruise on his face, right by his jaw, a really nasty-looking one. I wonder what happened to him, if he's okay.

I have to snap out of this—whatever I feel around him. "Lucky me. And stop calling me Hortense."

"But I thinks it kind of suits you. And seriously, I was."

"It does not suit me. And you thinking about me means what? That there're three girls in town now instead of two?"

"Close. Five."

I laugh before I can stop myself. He grins at me. "I was surprised to see you last night, you know. I didn't figure you for a yacht-club-party kind of girl."

"How would you know?"

"What, you don't think I get invited to yacht club parties?"

I look at him.

"Yeah, okay, I don't. It's just that you just seem too—"

"What?" I say, tensing, aware that I'm talking to a cop. And cute or not, that's something I really shouldn't be doing.

"Nice. But I don't know why I was thinking that."

"Yeah. Great seeing you again." I turn back around. The guy with the screaming kids has finally reached the counter.

"Okay," he says. "Truth? You're like, too alive for those kind of parties. There's something about you. A spark."

I turn back around. My insides are doing that fluttery thing again. "A spark?"

"Yeah."

I stare at him, unsure of what to say.

"Never mind," he says, blushing a little. "It's early. I haven't had my soda yet."

"What?"

"You know. Soda. Bubbles, lots of sugar to rot your teeth. Great stuff."

"You drink soda in the morning?"

"Now you sound like my dentist."

"It's just—well, I do too. But the first time I came in here and asked for one they—"

"Made you take the walk of shame, right?"

"The what?"

"You know, over to the case." He points to the corner. "Asking you if you want a glass of milk on your way there. The usual."

I laugh. "Walk of shame? Yeah, I had to do that."

"What about the milk? They did ask you if you wanted milk instead, right?"

I shake my head.

"Ruthie," he calls out, and an older woman behind the counter turns around. "I hope you know I have proof you're picking on me. I was just talking to Hortense here, and she doesn't get hassled about milk when she orders soda."

I feel my face turn red as everyone—and I mean everyone—turns to look at us. And you know the worst part? Not one person says "Hortense? That's such an obviously fake name."

Oh God, I look like a Hortense. I glance over at him. "Do you pick on everyone like this?"

"What?" he says. "Pick on? Ruthie loves me. Don't you, Ruthie?"

"Like the plague," Ruthie says. "What happened to your face?"

"Broke up a bar fight."

Ruthie laughs.

"What? I could have."

"Sure," Ruthie says, still laughing, and finally it's my turn at the counter.

"You don't want that one," Ruthie tells me as I'm pointing at the cream-filled donuts. "You want this one instead."

"I really would rather have—"

"Trust me," she says. "And you," she tells Greg, "have got to stop trying to help Joanie out. She was in here earlier waving her hands around and worrying you'd broken your jaw getting hit with that stupid so-called portable steam tray."

"Hey, don't knock Joanie. She makes a mean lobster roll."

"Who do you think taught her how to do that? She's my daughter and I love her, but these fancy parties she's trying to do for the summer people after being a caterer for a month and a half? She's going to give herself a heart attack."

"She's not doing so bad," he says. "Really, Ruthie, she isn't. Last night, the whole problem was traffic. That's all. Tell her not to worry, okay? And don't you worry either."

"I don't worry. I'm too busy making these goddamned donuts."

"Right, right. I forgot. I just meant that if you were thinking about worrying, you didn't need to."

Ruthie waves a hand at him and grumbles something under her breath, but I see her smile as she turns away.

When I try to pay for my donuts Greg won't let me, tells the girl working behind the counter that no, he owes me and the last time he didn't pay up I clocked him one.

"See?" he says, showing her his jaw.

She laughs and takes the twenty he hands over, clearly thinking he's the greatest thing ever. I decide I don't like her and turn away. I hope Ruthie didn't give me some sort of weird flavored cream donut. I hate the ones with the "special" fillings.

"Don't forget your soda," the girl calls out.

Crap, the soda. I turn back around, head toward the case. Greg is already there, holding two cans.

"Here," he says, and holds one out to me.

"Maybe I don't want that. Maybe I want—" The only other kind of soda they have is diet. Ick. Oh well. "A diet."

"Yeah, the look of distaste on your face really has me convinced. Besides, have you seen what's in the stuff? It'll preserve you from the inside out."

"That's what I always tell my mother."

"Oh yeah?" He waves the soda at me.

Damn. If Mom were here she'd be so pissed at me. I'm not supposed to mention I even have a mother. "Like I can drink that now. Maybe if you shake it a little more it'll explode before I even get a chance to open it."

"Hey, where's your sense of adventure?"

"In the car."

He laughs, then hands me the unshaken can. "Okay, here you go."

"Thanks." I turn to leave.

"Hey, do you—can you stay for a while?"

"What? Why?"

"Do you know you almost always answer a question with another question?"

"Is that a problem?"

He grins. "No. I'm just saying, that's all. It's actually very interesting." He sits down at a table, motions at the seat across from him. "You want to sit down?"

"With you?"

"And again with the questions. Yeah, with me. You should give me a chance. I've been told I grow on people."

"What, like fungus?"

He laughs. "Something like that."

"Hey, Hortense," Ruthie calls out. "Sit down and eat with the poor boy already, will you? I win a buck if you do."

"Ruthie," Greg says, "I knew there was a reason why I love you. The continual public humiliation is such a joy, really."

"Hey, at least I bet on you."

"That's true. Who bet against me?"

Ruthie looks at her coworkers. The three other women making donuts raise their hands.

"Oh, come on," he says, "I'm not that—oh, forget it." He looks at me. "I don't suppose you're willing to let poor Ruthie win a buck."

I look at Ruthie and then back at him. I sit down. Ruthie grins, and I watch her collect her money.

"See, she's not so bad," he says, and then, pitching his voice a little louder, "for a battle-axe."

"Don't think I won't come over there and kick your ass," Ruthie says. "And tell your mother she needs to call Stan about the reunion."

"I'm not a messenger service," he says.

Ruthie glares at him.

He grins at her. "I'll tell her, I promise."

"You've lived here forever, haven't you?" I ask, fascinated. I've never known someone who's lived in one place their whole life.

"No," he says, surprised. "Why would you—oh, because of Ruthie? She's my mom's cousin and she has lived here forever. I moved here about a year ago."

"Because you wanted to be a cop?"

"Yeah. That and if I worked here I'd get to live

near the beach. I like the ocean."

"Why?"

"I knew you'd go back to the questions. What do you mean, why? Who doesn't like the ocean?"

"It's just water."

"So then why are you living here?"

"You have to like the ocean in order to live here?"

"You know, one of these days we're going to have an actual conversation."

He grins at me, and I find myself grinning back. "I can just imagine how thrilling that would be."

"See, progress already! That wasn't even a question. In fact—oh hell. It's after nine? Damn."

After nine? I look around and sure enough, the donut-shaped clock on the wall says it is. Mom is going to be mad. Shit. "I gotta go."

"Yeah, me too," he says. "I'm gonna be late for work. But hey, it was really nice running into you."

I look at him. My heart is suddenly pounding really hard.

"No chance of getting that in reply, is there?" he asks.

"Nope," I say, and hope my voice sounds normal. "But thanks for the donuts. And the soda."

"Anytime. I mean, I am still waiting for a name, you know."

"Bye."

"Hey, was that a smile?"

Yes. "No."

"Sorry, my mistake. It was a definite frown. Pretty, though."

I look at him. He shrugs and then stands up. "What? It is."

He thinks I have a pretty smile. "I—uh—look, thanks for the food, okay? But I'm not—you're just—I can't—"

"Oh. Is it because—I saw you with that guy last night. Are you two . . . together?"

Yes. That's what I should say. Instead I shake my head.

"Oh," he says, and grins. "That's nice to know. Maybe—"

"I really do have to go," I tell him. I feel weird. I want him to keep talking. I'm very sure that I shouldn't.

"Right," he says, and grins at me, a crooked sad little smile. "Me too. I'll see you around, Hortense."

I watch him leave. I like talking to him. I really do. But he's a cop.

"A cop," I mutter to myself, and get up. I have to remember that. I drive back to the house, back to Mom and everything that's familiar.

12

Mom's gone when I get back, a scribbled note telling me she'll see me later. There's nothing angry in it, nothing about missing donuts or anything, and I know that means she left soon after I did, probably forgetting I was out picking up something for her.

Upstairs I find one of those free real estate guides lying on her bed, a red circle around one of the entries. She must have seen it and decided to pay Harold a visit. I sit down and read the whole thing: house for rent, two bedrooms, water view, right by an ocean inlet, blah blah blah. The person listed as contact is—yep, that's right, Harold. I bet we'll be moving real soon.

I pack up my things and most of Mom's. Under the pile of maps she's been working with is a piece of paper with a list of names on it. Maid to Order, Merry Maids, that sort of thing. I can guess what's coming. We've never done anything exactly like it before, but going in as a maid to snag the silver is a good option, a smart one. I can't think of any reason why it wouldn't work.

This means in a few days Sydney will be gone and someone else will take her place. We won't need any more information and I'll become someone who will do—well, whatever Mom tells me to. Someone who won't have time for the beach, for hanging out. It's for the best and I know it. I can't keep talking—really talking—to someone I'm going to steal from. I should be able to but I just . . . I don't like how it makes me feel.

I leave the house, go for a walk. I head toward the public beach but don't go there. Instead I stop at a convenience store at the beginning of the tourist strip and grab a bottle of water.

"Sydney?"

"Allison?" What is she doing here?

"Hey!" She grins. "I didn't expect to see you."

"Same here."

"I'm just—well"—she lowers her voice—"I

thought Brad might, I don't know, be here. I know it's dumb but he lives nearby, so . . ." She blushes. "How about you?"

"Just out for a walk."

"Everything okay? You look a little—"

"I'm fine."

"Really?"

I nod.

"You know what?" she says. "You should totally come to my house for dinner."

"What?" Dinner? Inside the Donaldson house? That would make Mom's year.

"It'll be fun. Well, not like wild party fun or anything. But you get to watch my dad try to light the grill, which is always hysterical."

"I—well, the thing is, I—" I can almost hear Mom hissing "Go!" in my ear.

"Filled up on water?" Allison laughs. "Besides, you never did tell me where you got your dress."

"Okay, I'll come." I tell myself I'm going because I have to, because Mom would want me to. But I'm not. I'm not going because of Mom. I'm going because I want to. I'm going because I want to have dinner with a friend. I've never done that before.

* * *

The house is exactly like it is in the pamphlet Mom and I have gone through, and I see rooms I know, rooms that I've studied. I see silver laid out in the open, resting on what looks like a dining room table.

I don't go near it. I don't want to. Instead I walk outside with Allison, head across a perfect lawn. I should be guessing how long it is, looking for security lights, for motion sensors. Instead I talk to her about Brad and suntans and shoes.

Her family is nice. Her mother and father are distracted but polite, shake my hand and offer me something to drink, ask about school. I tell them the story I told Allison the day we met and then realize James has arrived and that he and Allison are talking. Arguing, actually.

"I don't need you deciding things for me," Allison says, her voice rising. "I'm eighteen. I can—and I know this is a shock for you—make up my own mind, James."

"Do we really have to talk about this now, Ally?"

"No, because you're going to mind your own business and let me lead my own life." She turns to me. "I mean, that's not too much to ask for, right, Sydney?"

"Absolutely," I say, and she grins at me.

"I'm just trying to look out for you," James says.

"Are you?" Allison says, voice suddenly sharp. "I would think you'd be too busy looking out for yourself."

"Allison, James, keep your voices down, please," their mother says. "In fact, both of you come with me—your father is attempting to light the grill and we all know what that means."

Both James and Allison laugh, the tension between them broken. "Come on," Allison says. "James and I will have to save him from himself and possibly run and get the fire extinguisher."

"I'll be right there," I say, and watch them go. I can have tonight, just a few hours I'll keep to myself. I'll be careful. I won't forget why I am really here. There is silver in this house and I saw it. I know I will see it again. Silver is the story of my life.

It is how Mom and I ended up here.

When I was little Mom did stuff she wouldn't touch now. She and Dad stole jewels, paintings, credit cards, basically anything they could get their hands on. But then Dad got arrested and Mom got worried. They'd never gotten married but I was around, proof of a connection between them.

I suppose I shouldn't say she was worried. Mom was angry. When I think back to what I remember most clearly about her then it's that she was always in motion—pacing around whatever apartment we were living in, tossing our things into paper bags and telling me to get in the car. We were constantly on the move and had nothing to show for it. I remember a series of uniforms—waitress, I guess, Mom going back to what she'd once known—and food brought home in grease-stained bags.

"This isn't living," she said one night as I was eating and she was pacing around the room. "I've got nothing now. Nothing. I need—"

I swallowed and watched her turn toward me, eyes shining.

We moved again and the uniforms stopped. Mom was home now, all the time, and one night we went for a drive, stopped, and walked to a large house. We stood in the shadows and waited for a long while. "Not a sound, baby," Mom whispered, and her fingers slid over my ear in a way I knew like breathing. I waited—and worried—but Mom came back and the next day I had new clothes and a new doll and Mom was happy.

Getting into silver was an accident. One night she went inside a house and paused before going upstairs to where a safe with jewels was supposed to be. I saw her through the window I was waiting by, watched her walk into a dining room and open a cabinet. Crammed inside were boxes full of silver forks and knives and spoons. There were other things too: teapots, candlesticks, serving trays. Mom took it all.

She let me look at it later, happiness lighting up her face as she did, and for once we didn't leave right away. We stayed and she checked the papers every day. It took a week and an overzealous housekeeper looking for something to do before anyone noticed the silver was gone. It got a paragraph in the paper and nothing more, didn't even make it onto the front page. Silver gone, burglary suspected, insurance claim filed. End of story.

"Silver," Mom told me, said the word like it was magic, and ever since it's ruled her. Ruled us. It's easy enough to find if you know where to look, and it's not high-profile enough to attract a lot of public attention. And anything that isn't high-profile is always easier to fence.

Because of silver I can pry the molding off a window without making a sound. I know how to test for plate even though I don't usually need to. I can drive a car, climb into a house, deal with growling dogs. I know exactly how much your average nineteenth-century tea service weighs—in troy ounces, even—and how many pieces it has.

For silver I learned to read, write, work numbers. For silver I learned the names of every plantation from Virginia to Florida. I can tell you which ones we've visited, which ones we want to, which ones we never will. I can tell you how to find someone's house no matter where it is. I can tell you what to do if there is silver inside.

The story of my life can be told in silver: in chocolate mills, serving spoons, and services for twelve. The story of my life has nothing to do with me. The story of my life is things. Things that aren't mine, that won't ever be mine. It's all I've ever known.

I wish it wasn't.

I can't stay here. I want to, want to eat hamburgers and talk about the beach. I want to help Allison plan ways to see Brad again. I want to be just like everyone else, but I can't because I'm not. I won't ever be.

I walk back to the house. Allison catches up to me as I'm heading for the door.

"Are you sneaking out?" She laughs. "I promise, despite the production with the grill—you really should have seen it—dinner will be edible. Daddy's just allowed to light it. Our cook wouldn't actually let him cook anything."

"I'm not feeling very well." I feel bad for her, for how she's standing there so trusting, so . . . so secure in what she knows, so sure of what she sees. I envy her. I wish I could feel that way, have that kind of life.

"Oh no," Allison says. "Do you need anything? Do you want me to drive you home? Let me just grab my keys and—"

I shake my head. "Tell everyone I said good-bye, okay?" My voice is so level, so polite.

"Okay," Allison says, puzzled-sounding. She calls out, "Bye, Sydney!" as I'm heading down the driveway. I don't turn around. It's not me she's calling. It's just a name, a name belonging to someone she thinks she knows. Someone who doesn't really exist.

Mom isn't back when I get home. I cry in the shower anyway, habit. Mom doesn't like it when I cry. When I was a kid she'd look at me, bewildered and then impatient if I didn't stop. Older, and she'd ask me why I was crying, listen to me sob out an explanation, and then say, "But baby, what does crying do? What does it change?"

"I cried over your father," she told me two days after I'd woken up from having sex with Roger and heard him and Mom out in the hall. I hadn't spoken to her since I'd said "Stop," and when I looked over at her she'd looked nervous. Unsure.

I'd always known I was a planet orbiting her bright star and that I was lucky she wanted me with her, that she'd kept me by her side. I'd always thought of her in terms of how much I loved her. I'd always been afraid that maybe she didn't love me.

But she did. She does. I saw that then. And so I said, "Really?"

"Yeah," she said. "I really . . . I loved him. He was my world and then he was gone and—" Her voice cracked a little and she cleared her throat. "But you know what? No one is everything, baby. Promise me you'll remember that. I don't want—" She reached out, ran a hand down my hair. "I don't want that for you, you understand me? I want you to always remember what you can believe in, remember that it's what—"

"What you can hold in your hands," I said, and watched her nod. When she did, I realized I hadn't cried over Roger. I realized I wasn't going to. I realized Mom had done what she did because she thought she was protecting me. She'd seen what I felt for Roger and saw what I couldn't, saw him for the jerk he was and tried as best she could, in the ways she knew how, to let me see it too and make sure I ended up in one piece. She didn't want me to be where she'd been, in the place where you cried and meant it.

What she'd done was awful, but she hadn't done it to hurt me. I'd hurt myself and she'd let me see that I could, showed me that I always had to be careful. And I have been since then. I have been careful, so careful. Too careful, I know Mom thinks, but she's wrong.

I haven't been careful enough because I stand in

the shower and cry for what I've never had and never will. A real home. Things I can truly call my own and keep forever. Friends. I am in the place where you cry and mean it.

It sucks.

13

Mom gets back late, very late, and she isn't alone. I hear footsteps crossing through the house with hers.

"I don't usually do this," Mom says, a giddy note in her voice that, if I didn't know better, I would think is real. She starts to say something else but then coughs. I wish she'd just go to the doctor already. I'll get her some cough syrup tomorrow. Maybe that will help.

Whoever she's with mumbles something in reply, voice low and drunken-sounding, ". . . sure your roommate isn't home?"

Roommate? Must be someone recently divorced and gun-shy about being with someone who has kids, even one who is eighteen. I'll have to remember, if he's still around in the morning, to call Mom—damn, what's her name again? Miranda, that's it. Miranda.

"No, no, she isn't," Mom says. "It's just you and me, Harold."

Harold. Of course. He mumbles something else and Mom laughs the way she does when someone says something she's heard a million times before but is acting like it's the first time.

"I can't thank you enough for everything you've done for me," she says. "You're . . . perfect. You're so perfect."

I roll my eyes. How could anyone fall for that?

Harold does, apparently, because he laughs, pleased-sounding, and then there are other noises. I pull my pillow over my head.

When I get up the next morning Mom is downstairs fiddling with the coffeemaker and Harold is gone.

"Hey, Miranda," I say anyway. "I just wanted to let you know my half of the rent is going to be real late this month. That's not a problem, right?"

"Funny," she says, and grins at me. "His third divorce was finalized a month ago. You would not believe what I had to do to get that man to take me to dinner."

"I can imagine," I say, and launch into an imitation of her voice last night. "'You're . . . perfect. You're so perfect.'"

"I know, I know. But people hear and see what they want to, baby. You know that. And did you hear him afterward? I had to—"

"Mom, please. I heard more than enough last night."

She rolls her eyes and then makes a face at the coffeemaker. "Baby, I can't get this to work. Will you fix me a cup of coffee? Please?"

I nod.

"I got us a house," she says, grinning. "We can move in this afternoon. And then," she says, getting up and coming over to me, sliding one arm around my shoulders, "things will finally start to happen."

I finish putting water in the coffeemaker and turn it on.

"Isn't that good?" she says, squeezing my arm gently, and I look at her. She's watching me intently. I force a smile.

"It's great. You want me to make you some toast or something?"

* * *

We're settled into the new house by midafternoon. It's past the public beach and the small houses that dot it, lies at the end of a dirt road by an inlet.

I love the house. From the moment we see it, I love it. It's small and low to the ground, brown wood and stone surrounded by rocks and trees. It's two stories and only five rooms, a living room and kitchen/dining room on the first floor, two bedrooms and a bath on the second. It's nothing special, but you can tell people live here. Mom doesn't like that at all, grimaces over the knickknacks the owners have left behind, framed pictures of boats and dogs and yellowing images that must be deceased relatives. She says the furniture, just about all of which is made of the same dark wood as the house, is "a disaster."

"Who thinks something like this"—she points at a chair, rough-hewn and angled to look out a bank of windows in the living room—"needs a pillow covered with tiny blue flowers? I'm afraid to even look in the bedrooms."

"At least you got a good deal on it," I say, and she sighs, drops her bag on the floor.

"At least it won't be for very long. Just looking around this place makes me want a stiff drink. In fact, I'm going to go get one. You want to come?"

I shake my head. When she's gone I pick up one of the pictures and pretend I know it, invent a world where I look out a window and know the view is something I can see for as long as I want, for forever if I choose.

I wake up really early the next morning because Mom's coughing yet again. She sounds terrible. I go check on her, see if she's awake, but of course she's still asleep. I figure I'll go ahead and get up, make her coffee. It turns out we're out of coffee and pretty much everything else, so I get dressed and head into West Hill.

In the grocery store I grab food for me and coffee for Mom, then head over to the aisle lined with cold remedies. I know she won't go see a doctor. In fact, I'm not sure Mom has ever been. I don't remember any visits.

I've only ever been twice—once when I got poison ivy so bad my eyes swelled shut (the woods in parts of Connecticut are a bitch) and once to have my arm stitched up after that stupid poodle bit it. We had to drive a hundred miles before Mom felt it was safe enough to stop, and I'd lost so much blood that all I remember is waking up and seeing a nice even row of stitches wrapping across my wrist and part way up my arm. The scar was hideously obvious for years, a deep bruised red, but it's faded now, a pale line racing across my skin.

I didn't think it would be difficult to buy cough syrup, but then I didn't realize there were about forty different kinds. Cough suppressant. Cough expectorant. Six-hour, eight-hour, all-day.

"Hortense, you sick?"

I look over, see Greg standing there dressed in jeans and a T-shirt, his cop shirt open over it. His last name is apparently Tollver. I'm happy to see him. Not a good sign.

"Stop calling me that."

"What else am I supposed to call you?"

I ignore him and pick up another bottle. Bubble-gum flavored? I can just imagine what Mom would say to that. I put it back down.

"Seriously, Hortense, are you sick?"

I gesture at his "outfit" and pick up another bottle. "They let you go to work dressed like that?"

"No, they let me leave work dressed like this,

Hortense. Trust me, you don't want that kind."

When I look over at him again he's grinning, and I can tell he's totally aware of how much I hate the stupid name he's given me. I look at the bottle I'm holding. It's "zany grape!" flavored and is actually for children. I put it in my cart. "Shows how much you know."

"Hortense," he says, and I can actually hear my teeth grinding together, "while you seem like a zany grape kind of girl, I doubt even you want a bottle that's leaking." He reaches over and takes it out of the cart. Purple goo is everywhere.

"Damn."

"How about this, Hortense?" He holds up a bottle of ordinary enough looking cough syrup. "It's even on sale this week, Hortense."

That's it. I can't stand that stupid name. "Danielle," I say, and yank the bottle out of his hand. "And it isn't on sale, you jackass. The one next to it is."

"Really?" he says, and looks closer at the shelf. "You're right. Sorry about that. So . . . Danielle, huh? You know, you kind of look like a Danielle."

Crap. Crap, crap, crap. My name isn't supposed to be shared with anyone, ever. And especially not with a cop. Now what do I do? Say it's not my real name? No, that would be stupid. And suspicious. Better to act like it's not a big deal. "You also thought I look like a Hortense."

"Nah. Nobody looks like a Hortense. Well, maybe she does." He points at a woman in a lime green jogging suit. "But you look like a Danielle. Or—" He tilts his head a little to one side. "A Dani."

I stare at him, forgetting about the cough syrup and my monumental screwup for a moment. I have always thought of myself as a Dani. Or, well, I've wanted to be. If I ever became the kind of person who could run around using my real name. Danielle seems so not me, is someone who lives in a house with a white ruffled bed and a cat named Fluffy.

But Dani, that seems like someone I could be. Dani would have an apartment with a comfy sofa. She'd have a dog and a job and all that normal life stuff.

"I knew I'd figure it out eventually," he says, and smiles. I almost—almost—start to smile back because it's nice to know I'm not the only person who thinks I could be a Dani, and because his smile makes me want to smile too, but then I catch a glimpse of a patch on his sleeve, one that spells out p-o-l-i-c-e.

"You haven't figured out anything except how to be annoying."

"See, I'm ignoring that because I know you don't really mean it."

"You definitely haven't figured out mind reading."

He laughs. "That's probably true. So, how's your mom doing?"

"What?" I'm stunned for a second and then remember that I mentioned her the other day. First Mom, now my name. This keeps getting worse and worse.

"Well, you seem fine. Annoyed, but fine. So I figure . . ." He gestures at the cough syrup.

"Yeah, it's for her." I try and think of something else to say, something that will change the subject and last just long enough for me to leave without looking like I'm trying to leave. "What are you doing here?"

"I love hanging out in grocery stores with paranoid women."

I stare at him. He laughs again and says, "I'm just following up on something. We got a call from someone at a party—the one you were at, actually—claiming one of the catering crew was taking purses out of the coat-check room. The guy works here, so

I stopped by to see when he's working again."

"Taking purses? Really?" Mom always likes to know if anyone else is working the area.

He looks at me, eyebrows raised, and I clear my throat. "I mean, I didn't realize that crime was a . . . thing around here."

"Once in a while." He runs a hand through his hair, making it stick up even more than it already is. "I don't suppose you saw anything at the party."

"Like what?"

He grins. "Like what we were just talking about. The coat-check room, remember?"

"Why would I be hanging around there?" I say. "It was a party. I was having fun. Besides, if someone was taking purses, all they'd get would be lipsticks and maybe a couple of compacts—nothing worth the time. If anyone was working the coatroom, chances are they were looking for keys."

"Keys? But . . . oh shit. Keys! Of course."

"Exactly," I say. "And if they were dumb enough to be seen, it's probably house keys and they were probably stupid enough to have them copied nearby. If they were smart, they'd have just taken car keys from the valet stand, copied them, and then put them back, because if you snatched the keys for say, five cars, and then spread stealing them out over a couple of weeks to avoid paperwork for the same kind of crime crossing anyone's desk—well, given the kind of cars around Heaven, you could make a lot of . . ."

I trail off because he's staring wide-eyed at me. Why did I just say everything I did? Why? What is it about him that makes me so . . . well, stupid? "I mean, I'm just saying. It's a theory."

"It's actually a really good one."

"Um. Thanks." The only thing I am actually thankful for right now—and believe me, it's a small thing—is that Mom isn't here because if she was . . . I don't even want to think about how mad she'd be. I might as well have just taped a sign to my head that says, "Hi! I'm a criminal! Ask me how you can be one too!"

"So, what are you doing today?"

"What?" Why does he want to know that?

"Today," he says. "What are you doing?"

"Well, I'm, uh, going home and"—I point at the cart—"I'll put the groceries away, make Mom take some cough syrup. Probably make a peanut butter sandwich and . . . um. Well, eat it."

He grins at me. "Have you ever been to Edge Island?"

"Edge Island?" Why is he asking me about an island?

"Yeah. It's not that far away—just an hour or so on the ferry. I was thinking that maybe, since you've only got the sandwich-making plans and all, you might want to go."

I look at him. He looks . . . kind of nervous. I don't get it. "You want me to go to an island with you?"

"Is this going to turn into a big extended question thing? I mean, if I say, 'Yeah, with me,' will you say, 'What do you mean by "with me"?'"

"Why would it turn into a question thing?"

He grins at me. "I don't know. Why would it?"

That grin again. I wish . . .

Wait a minute. "Are you trying to ask me out?"

"At any point during any conversation we'll have is there a chance that you won't reply to everything I say with questions?"

"So you weren't trying to ask me out?"

"I want you to know you're doing wonders for my self-esteem here. Which means, before you ask another question, yes, I was. I mean, I am."

"Really?" No one's ever asked me out before. Hit on me, sure. Groped me, absolutely. But asked me for a date? Never.

"What else would I be doing? See, now you've got me doing it too."

"What would you have done if I said yes?" I shouldn't be doing this, I know, but I really want to hear his answer.

"Probably asked you to repeat yourself in the form of a question since it'd be the only way I could be sure of your answer. And look, I really am sorry. I didn't mean to make you uncomfortable or anything."

"So you don't want to go?"

"Are you saying you do?"

"What if I am?"

"You know, I don't have a question to reply with here, so I guess if you're saying 'yes' in your own special way, we could meet back here—well, not here, in the middle of the store where people are walking by and looking at us but not saying hello—yes, I'm talking about you, Mrs. Reynolds, how are you?—but in the parking lot. In like an hour?"

"An hour." He wants to go out with me!

"Yeah. So you can drive home and put your"—he

looks into the cart—"genuine artificial cheddar flavor soy protein snack crackers away. And pass out cough syrup."

"It doesn't really say genuine artificial cheddar flavor."

"It does." He points at the bag. "So I'll see you? In like an hour?"

"So we can take a ferry ride to an island?"

"Well, yeah," he says. "But we could also, I don't know, talk or something."

"Sure, I'll meet you in an hour," I tell him, heart pounding because I shouldn't do this but I want to.

And because I'm going to.

14

I go home and put everything away. Mom comes downstairs, stops in the living room, and stands staring at me, one hand resting on the sofa.

"What's up?" I ask.

"You look a little flushed. Are you feeling okay?"

"Yeah. I'm going out for a while, but I'll take a cab, leave the car here."

"No, take the car. I'm going to stay in today. This stupid cold . . ." She shakes her head. "It's disgusting. I can hear stuff sloshing around when I breathe."

"When you breathe?"

"Yes. You want me to describe my phlegm to you or something?"

"Oh yes, please. Look, if you've got stuff in there, maybe it's the kind of thing that a doctor—"

"It's not a big deal. It just feels strange. Is there any coffee?"

"Just started a pot. While you're waiting, you can have some cough syrup." I wave the bottle at her.

"Ugh. If I say no, are you going to dump it into my coffee?"

"What do you think?"

Mom sighs. "Fine. I'll take some."

"Now?"

"Honestly, Danielle."

"Just take it. You wouldn't believe what I had to go through to get it."

Mom pours some syrup into the little dosage cup and takes it. She grimaces, then hands the whole thing back to me. "What you had to go through to get it?"

I open my mouth to tell her about Greg but all that comes out is, "It's a long story. A long, boring story."

"Well, then I definitely want to hear it."

"Funny. Going now. Don't forget to take more of this." I pick up the bottle, look at the label. "Every four hours, okay?"

"Absolutely," Mom says, and I know that means I'll come back to find the bottle exactly as full as it is right now. I sigh, lean over, and kiss her cheek.

"I'll see you later."

She waves at me over one shoulder, already turned away and watching the coffeemaker, just waiting for that first cup to brew. I leave and drive back to the grocery store. For my "date." With a cop.

I park pretty far away—it's bad enough he's seen the car once already—and walk to the store. Greg's there, and his car isn't what I figured a cop's non-cop car would be like. For one thing, it's a station wagon. For another, the back bumper is covered with stickers, all for bands I've never heard of. Cops always drive horribly practical sedans or huge pickup trucks/SUVs, and they never have bumper stickers. At least not like these.

"This is your car?"

"Uh oh, jumping straight into questions. This can't be good. You don't like it?"

"No, it's actually—it's just not what I thought you would drive."

He laughs. "You know what? I figured you'd take one look and say it matches my hair or something."

I look over at him. "Well, now that you mention it . . ."

He grins and I grin back. I tell myself I'm only doing that because I have to. I mean, someone smiles at you, you're supposed to smile back. The fact that I want to isn't important.

"Ready to go?"

I nod, and get in the car. I've never been in a station wagon before, or at least not one like this, with its bumper stickers and signs of its owner's personality everywhere.

I've also never been on a date.

Or gone somewhere voluntarily with a cop.

"You okay?" he says. "You seem a little worried. I know the car doesn't look like much, but it runs really well."

I nod again, and notice I'm twisting my hands together in my lap, like I'm nervous. Which I am, but I know better than to show it. Why did I agree to this again?

He glances at me, gaze lingering on my arms for a moment—I force myself to still my hands—and then starts the car.

"See?" he says, grinning, and I know exactly why

I agreed to this.

I want to be here.

"So, what happened?" he asks as we pull out of the parking lot.

"With what?"

"Your arm. You've got a wicked scar."

"What?" I clear my throat, thinking of the dog that bit me. Of why the dog bit me. Of just why I really shouldn't have agreed to this, no matter how much I want to be here. "You—you want to know what happened to my arm?"

"Well, yeah. If you want to talk about it, that is. I mean, I'm pretty sure I know what happened but . . ."

He knows? How could he know? Unless—I look over at him. Does he know who I am? Who I really am?

"It's okay," he says, his voice gentle. "I understand."

He holds his right arm out toward me. At first I don't see anything but then I look closer, see a series of faint thin white lines crossing his wrist.

"Oh. You got bit by a dog too?"

"I—wait. You got bit by a dog?"

"Yeah, a poodle. And before you laugh . . ." I look

over at him. He's not laughing. In fact, he looks kind of stunned.

I look at his arm again. I look at him.

I look at him, and I understand what happened.

I met a girl worth three quarters of a billion dollars at a party once. She had the saddest eyes of anyone I've ever met and a row of white lines on her wrists, scars so thick her skin was just a faint tinge under them.

"You—" I don't quite know what to say. I mean, I do—you tried to kill yourself—but his expression is this weird mix of pain and embarrassment and what looks like a kind of angry fear, and what I end up saying is, "You have them on your other arm too."

He doesn't say anything, doesn't even move, but then he slowly nods. *Yes.* When he does, I lean over and touch my fingers to his wrist because I know how it feels to have to live with something you wish wasn't true.

"I was fifteen," he says quietly. "It happened just after my dad died. He was driving home, pulled over to help what he thought was someone with a flat tire, and got shot."

"Shot?"

"Yeah. He was just in the wrong place at the wrong time. The thing is, the last time I saw him we'd fought. He'd found drugs in my room and went crazy, said all the things cops do—'Drugs kill, you don't know what I see'—all that stuff. I told him he was full of shit; I hated that he was a cop, hated what everyone thought it meant about him, about me—it was like it defined all of us. I told him that, he died, and I thought . . ."

He drums his fingers on the steering wheel. "I kept thinking about what I'd said to him, about what he'd said to me. So, the day after the funeral, I took all the drugs I had and then opened a package of razor blades. I don't even remember doing it, I was so gone. Dad's partner found me. He'd come over to see how Mom was doing, came back to my room to talk to me. I was so fucked up I didn't do a very good job, just hacked my skin up, mostly, and so he patched me up, had a doctor friend of his come over and check on me later so I wouldn't have to go to the hospital. So Mom wouldn't have to go back to the hospital."

He blows out a deep breath. "I've—I've never told anyone about it before. I just . . . I thought you—"

"My father's gone too. Not dead, but he might as

well be. So I—I know I don't understand, not really. But I do know what it's like to lose someone. I know how much it hurts when you don't get to say good-bye the way you wish you could have."

He nods. "You know what I remember most? Not the funeral, not even the moment when the doctor came in and told us Dad was gone. I remember what Mom said to me when I woke up afterward, how she checked my wrists and then said, 'I want to tell you a story.' She told me about Dad's first case. He found a thirteen-year-old dead from an overdose—no witnesses, no nothing, just a dead kid. They couldn't even find someone to claim the body. He told her about it when he got home and she said all the stuff people say, that it's so sad, so terrible. She asked him how he could handle knowing things like that would happen over and over again, how he could deal with the world being like that. And he said, 'Maybe I think the world can be different.' She said she thought I'd know what he meant."

"Do you think he's right?"

"I don't know. Sometimes I think that yeah, maybe. Other times . . . other times I'm not so sure. I think things aren't as simple as he thought—he was a cop cop, you know? Everything was either right or wrong for him, nothing in between. But he wanted to make things better, and that—that's something I can believe in. I just wish I'd seen it earlier. Before he was gone."

"I think . . . I think sometimes that's how it is. Sometimes people have to go before you—before you get stuff. Before you can really get it."

"Yeah," he says. "It sucks that they have to go in order for it to happen, though."

"But at least then you know," I say, and now I'm thinking of my father. "I mean, sometimes a person sticks around but might as well be gone, you know? They're there, but when you're with them what you get is so close to nothing it might as well be that."

"It could change, though. You've got that."

"Right, because when the first thing they ask is how long you'll be around, it just means they're afraid or something. It's such crap. It's just . . . it's all they can give. All they're willing to give. But the worst part is that you can't help thinking 'maybe' even though it's stupid and then, when they finally do go, you feel so hurt and . . ."

I trail off, and look out the window. I haven't said

this much about my father ever. Not even to Mom.

"I—"

"Don't tell me you feel sorry for me," I say, angry with him for bringing up stuff I don't like thinking about. Angry at myself for being so drawn to him. "'Sorry' is bullshit and it's always followed by more bullshit."

"You're right."

I look over at him, surprised.

"You are," he says. "It's all I heard after Dad died. Everyone was sorry, so sorry. After a couple of weeks, I never wanted to hear the word again. Things . . . well, things suck sometimes. And sometimes you can fix it. And sometimes you can't. It's just the way it is."

"Do you miss your dad?"

"Yeah. You?" He looks over at me, his crazy hair shining in the sun, and the understanding in his eyes makes my own sting a little.

"Yeah," I say. "I miss him."

There's a crowd of people waiting to get on the ferry, and as Greg and I join them I get elbowed by someone swinging around a video camera. Greg catches my arm when I stumble and suddenly we're standing very close to each other.

"Hey," he says, "you okay?" and for a second—just a second only, I swear—I wish he'd kiss me.

That scares me. It scares me a lot.

"I'm fine." I take a step back, putting some distance between us. "Do you think they'll actually let us on the boat soon, or will we have to stand here and stare at it for an hour or something?"

"Two hours. Three at the most."

"Oh, okay then," I say, and someone behind us yells, "Hey, I just heard they won't be letting us on the boat for three hours!" We grin at each other.

They do let us on the ferry eventually, and Greg and I end up standing out on the deck. It's loud: the slap of the ocean against the boat, the sound of the engine, the wind blowing all around us. We stand by the railing together, in silence, and it's not weird or anything. It's nice. Comfortable.

"We're almost there," he says after a while, leaning toward me. "This is my favorite part—the whole place just sort of suddenly comes into view."

I look out at the ocean. He's right. The island is a speck at first and then a larger one and then suddenly it's a place and I can see grass and homes and narrow winding roads.

"It's . . ." It's alone, one small island in the middle of the sea, and yet it doesn't look lonely. I've never seen anything like it.

"I know," he says. "Pretty amazing, isn't it?"

I nod and look over at him. He's looking back at me, a little smile on his face.

"What?" I say.

"Nothing."

"You're smiling."

"So? I smile all the time. Not like some people."

"What are you saying?"

"What do you think I'm saying?"

"I think you're a pain in the ass."

"There we go," he says. "I knew I could do it."

"Do what?"

"Make you smile."

"I'm not smiling," I tell him. But I am. I can feel it.

15

When we leave the ferry we walk up to what Greg tells me is "the town." It's nothing but stores and an amazing view.

"You want to look at anything?" he asks, pointing at the stores.

"Hell, no." I know a racket when I see one and I'm sure this "town" makes a fortune from people who run around buying things simply because they had to ride on a boat to get here.

"Okay, that wasn't even a question," Greg says. "We're definitely getting out of here." He starts walking, heading away from the stores and up a narrow road. I watch him for a second, just sort of . . . caught, I guess, by how easy it is to talk to him, to hang out with him.

"You coming?" he asks, looking back at me, and

then he grins. "Or are you checking out my ass?"

I roll my eyes and walk up to him. "Please. You don't have an ass."

"I knew you were checking it out! And I do so have—" He twists, looking back over his shoulder. "Well, okay, maybe not in these pants. But I do, really, I swear. And it's actually quite—"

"I so don't need to hear the rest of that sentence," I say, and start walking. He laughs and catches up to me.

We walk for a while. The road gets narrower and hillier. It's amazingly quiet. All I can hear is the ocean, the wind, and the occasional car, most of which are some kind of tourist taxi.

At first we also get passed by a lot of people on bicycles, but they start to thin out as we keep walking, and by the time we've walked up our fifth hill all I hear is the ocean and the wind and our footsteps.

"So where are we going?" I ask.

"You'll see."

"I'll see?"

"Yeah," he says. "You'll like it. Trust me."

I freeze. Trust. I hate that word. It doesn't mean a thing and I stop walking, all the misgivings I had about being here, about him, coming back. I should have known better than this.

"I'm not real good with trust."

"What? You?" he says, and looks back at me, eyebrows raised and a grin creasing his face. "I never would have guessed."

I should have known better than this, and the thing is . . . I do. I do know better. I should never have agreed to this, never should have thought I could go on a date with anyone, much less a cop. It was stupid to come here with him, and I should just get out of it now.

"You know what? This was a bad idea."

His grins fades. "What?"

"You heard me. This was a bad idea and I . . . why did you even bring me here?"

He's silent for a moment. "I wanted to."

"What?" Of all the things I thought he might say, that wasn't one of them. He wanted to bring me here.

I want to believe him. I want to so much it scares me, and I take a step back, away from him.

"Okay," he says. "I'm just going to walk—" He points off into the distance, and I can sort of make out a path. "If you want to come, that would be great, because the view is amazing and I think you'll like it. If not . . . well, there's a ferry that leaves in half an hour."

He fishes in his pockets, pulls out a ticket, and then holds it out toward me.

"And if I go?" I say. Here's where there will be a catch. Where something bad will happen. I know it will. It has to. It always does.

"You go. I won't be able to drive you anywhere when you get back, obviously, since I'll be . . ."—he points over at the path again—"but if you ask them to call a taxi for you when you board, they will."

I wait, but he doesn't say anything else.

"I don't understand what you want from me," I finally say.

"Yeah, I get that." He hands me the ticket, his fingers brushing against mine. "I don't want anything from you."

I stare at him. "Everyone wants something."

He shoves a hand through his hair. "Well, okay. I wanted to bring you here, like I said. And I wouldn't mind showing you the view. So I guess I do want something after all. I want to spend time with you. But not if you don't want to. So . . . " He turns away from me, walks up the road.

I watch him go and then look down at the ferry ticket in my hand.

When I'm halfway down the last hill we walked up, I turn around. I expect to see him behind me, but he's not there.

I don't get it. There has to be something more going on than him just wanting to spend time with me. Nothing can be that simple.

Can it?

I walk back up the hill, sure he'll appear now, but he doesn't. I reach the path and look down it. It's long and winding. I can see the sea from here but I can't see where the path ends. I can't see Greg either. I hesitate for a second, and then I start walking.

I find out why I couldn't see where the path ends when I'm about halfway down it. It basically disappears, looping back into the rock that makes up the island. I'm walking along a narrow ledge that looks like it will drop off into nothing when I round the next corner. Should I go on? I take a cautious step forward, then another, and then I bump into something. Someone.

"I guess I should have told you the path just kind

of ends," Greg says. He's sitting down, looking out at the ocean.

"What are you doing here?"

He looks up at me. "Shouldn't that be my question?"

It should, but I'm afraid to answer it. I turn away, staring out at the sea, and my breath catches.

I've seen the ocean up close before. It's nothing special, or so I've always thought. But this . . . it's not just a long dull blue-gray line stretching out toward the horizon. This is different. There's water everywhere, crashing noisily over rocks just a few feet below us, churning and rolling and alive. It's terrible and beautiful at the same time.

"Wow." I sit down on the ledge next to him. Now that I'm closer the water is even more mesmerizing; twisting and turning, fighting like it wants to get away from the rocks and then turning back, rushing toward them.

"Yeah," he says. "The first time I came here, I thought the whole place was—well, like it is in town. I was pissed I'd come out here because if I want to see expensive crap I can do that anytime and don't have to sit on a boat for an hour first. But then I walked around, and past all the crap are places like this. And they're everywhere, all over the island. This was the first one I found, though, and sometimes I come back just to sit and watch the ocean. I like it."

He's silent for a moment. "Did that sound as stupid as I think it did?"

"No. There's—there's something about it. Something . . ." I lean forward a little, and salt spray blows up over me, the ocean raining gently onto my skin. "I don't know what it is, though."

"Me either," he says, and leans forward too. I watch water spray across his hands, drops catching on his wrists and running over his palms, his fingers. And so we sit there, together, in silence, and watch the ocean roar.

We ride the ferry back from the island the same way we did to it, in silence standing on the deck, only this time we stand at the opposite end and watch the island fade smaller and smaller. He asks me if I want to stop and get something to eat as we're driving back to the grocery store and for a second I'm tempted, think of his face as he sat looking at the ocean, about how he didn't bullshit me with some story about what the view meant to him, about what it being there meant for the world, for me. He just said he liked it, and I like that.

I like him. And I can't. I shouldn't. "I've got to get home."

"Okay," he says, and we turn in to the grocery store parking lot. "Do you need a ride?"

"No. I'm fine."

He nods. "Well, I . . . thanks for coming with me."

I look over at him. The sun is just starting to set and it's caught his hair, gleams off it. "I guess I'll see you around."

"Oh yeah?" He grins.

"Now who's the question person?"

He laughs. "I'll see you later, Dani." I look at him for a second, the strangeness of being called that and the even stranger rightness of it washing over me. Then I get out of the car.

He waves before he pulls out onto the road. I watch him drive away and when he's almost out of sight, far enough away so I figure he can't see me, I let myself wave back.

16

Mom's waiting for me when I get home, sitting on the sofa eating soy crackers and grinning. I smell the reason for her grin as soon as I walk into the house.

"Pizza!"

"Yeah," she says. "I think I remember a certain someone liking it."

"You thought right." I sit down and eat two slices.

"You want any?" I ask when I'm done, looking at the six remaining slices.

"Maybe later."

I laugh then, and she says, "What? I might."

"Uh huh. I've never seen you eat pizza, you know. That's not normal."

"I'm plenty nor—" She breaks off, coughing.

"Did you take more cough medicine today? I'll go get it and—"

"Later. Right now we need to talk."

So we talk, or rather, she does. It turns out she spent the day checking maid services.

"Here," she tells me, and hands me a piece of paper with an address on it. I recognize it as being right outside Heaven. "This is the one we want. You've got an interview tomorrow."

"So do you want me to drive you or—wait. I've got an interview?"

"I've been out a lot, been seen a lot, and this is a small place, baby."

"You just don't want to clean toilets."

Mom laughs. "Maybe. But I also know the job will go better if you do it."

I look at her, unsure of what to say. It's not that I don't know that I'm pretty good at what we do—how could I not be? It's been my whole life, is my life, even if I've spent a lot of time wishing it wasn't. And to hear her say that a job will go better if I pull it, to know she trusts me that much . . . well, that should make me happy.

It doesn't. It makes me wonder what's wrong. I mean, I know Mom believes in me, in what she's taught me. But I also know who's the best at everything in this family. I know we both know that. And it isn't me.

"Quit looking at me like that," she says. "You'd think I'd never said anything nice to you before."

"It's not that. It's—"

"Go upstairs and bring the folder with all the papers down, okay?"

"Mom—"

She shakes the box of crackers at me. "You know, these are really good."

I sigh, knowing that's all I'm going to get out of her, and go upstairs. As I'm looking in her room for the folder I can hear her coughing again.

"You really need to take more cough syrup," I say when I'm back downstairs. She makes a face at me and I make a face right back, then go into the kitchen and grab the bottle off the counter—right where I left it this morning. I knew it. I make her take another dose, holding the folder just out of reach until she does.

"Quit it," she says, swatting at the folder. "You have the soul of a cranky old person, you know that? I swear, next thing you'll be telling me to pick up my room."

"Don't tempt me." I hand her the folder. She flips through it and then stops, pulls out two things and hands them to me.

Fake social security card and driver's license, all you need to become someone else long enough to hold a shitty job. I look them both over. "Rebecca, huh? Twenty years old. You know, one of these days I'm going to end up being someone who's my actual age."

"Only you would complain about being young," Mom says, and takes the cards away. "Social security number?"

I tell her. She nods. "Driver's license number and address?"

I tell her and she hands them back. "Good."

She tests me again during the night, waking me up four times to ask me my new name, social security number, and address. I am good at memorizing names and numbers quickly, just like I'm good at reading maps. I wonder what use any of it would do me if I didn't run around stealing things. Probably not much.

My interview—with a company called Maid to Order—is in the afternoon. It lasts longer than I thought it would and by the end I'm pretty sure I'm not going to get offered a job.

I'm glad about that. I shouldn't be, but I am because I don't think this place is good for me and Mom. Things don't feel like they usually do. I don't feel like I usually do. There's Greg, for one thing. I haven't told my mother everything—or even anything—about him although I know I should. A day spent with a cop isn't something to skip over, even if he did just want to show me a view.

I still can't get over that. He wanted to take me to the island just to take me there. He wanted to spend time with me.

I fold my hands together and look down at them resting in my lap, wait for the guy I'm talking to, Stu, to tell me, "Thank you," in the way that means, "That was half an hour I'll never get back."

"So I'll just get the tax forms, then."

I look up and Stu is holding out a hand for me to shake. "Oh," I say, and remember to tack on "Great!" at the last second.

Looks like I got myself a job.

By the time I leave, having filled out a bunch of forms and agreed to take a drug test at some facility an hour away in the morning—and yet I have to be at work by eight—I'm a brand-new employee. I even have a bright yellow uniform (cost subtracted from my paycheck, which, at the pitiful amount I was quoted, means I'll be making exactly squat) to show for it.

Mom is really happy, gets a kick out of the uniform, and even cancels a date with Harold to take me out to dinner. We go to some place she read about in a magazine, an hour away and in another state, and she's positively beaming by the time we're seated. I can't remember the last time I saw her smile like this for anything other than our fence counting out money.

"What's going on?" I ask, and she shakes her head, looks over at the table next to us, and smiles at the people sitting there—two guys, both clearly very happy to have her smile at them.

"I'm just happy, baby. And hey—" She taps my menu. "You should be happy too."

I look at her and she is looking back at me, still smiling but with a question shading her eyes.

"I am," I say, and tap her menu back. "What are you going to have?"

Two hours later, after a lot of flirting with the guys at the next table (Mom, not me) and a pretty crappy piece of fish followed by a very good chocolate mousse, I find out why Mom is so happy.

"Here," she says when we're in the car on the way back to the house, and hands me her purse. "Inside, zipper pocket."

I click on the overhead light. Inside the pocket is a newspaper clipping, an interview with Mrs. Donaldson. She talks about her community activities, donations and fund-raisers and all that stuff. Mention of her children, and I smile when she describes Allison as "joyful." Then the reporter asks about her anniversary party, and Mrs. Donaldson makes a very bad joke about celebrating marriage by serving dinner to 120 people.

"One hundred and twenty?" I ask. With an average place setting of three forks, a couple of knives, and two spoons . . . that's well over eight hundred pieces, and that doesn't even start to count serving trays and who knows what else.

"I know, baby. I knew this town was going to be good to us. I just knew it." Mom turns up the radio and starts singing along.

That's what she's so happy about. Silver. Of course. I don't know why I even wondered. But she's right to be happy. We'll be set for a long time after this.

I wait to feel happy too. I know I won't, not over this, not over silver, and I don't. I never do.

The less said about the first day of "work," the better. Let's just say that the rich leave as much junk lying around as everyone else does only they have a lot more rooms to leave it in. Also, if I ever see another marble shower—requiring special cleaner that smells so bad it makes my head ache and my vision spot green—it'll be too soon.

After our last house the crew I've been assigned to drives back to the office to hear a "motivational speech"—it seems Stu is big on those—and get tomorrow's assignments. Me, Joan (smokes a lot and very bossy), Maggie (saving every penny for her family back home; I thought that was nice the first eighteen times I heard it, then it got annoying), and Shelly (pregnant, and prone to discussing every symptom of morning sickness in graphic detail) are going to clean Williams, Sherrill, Stone, and Donaldson.

Donaldson. I knew it was coming, I did, but I just—I didn't think it would be so soon.

Mom makes a face when she picks me up. "You

smell like—God, what is that?"

"Marble cleaner. They're sending me to the Donaldson house tomorrow."

"Baby, that's great! I know we've got a floor plan, but still. Learn as much as you can about the security system because the next time you get sent back, we'll do it."

Yes. Sounds great. Sure thing. "I can't do it."

"You can't do it?" She looks away from the road, looks at me. "What the hell does that mean?"

"I met the daughter, remember? Allison. At the party. She introduced us. If she sees me at her house—"

"Oh baby, you talked to her for what, two minutes? And besides, girls like that don't notice maids. People only see what they want to see. You know that."

"But . . ."

"But what?"

But there's something else. I didn't tell you this before, Mom, but I've been to the Donaldson house. Allison invited me. I've talked to her for more than two minutes. I met her before the party. I've hung out with her. I've never done that with anyone we were going to rob before. I've never done that with anyone before.

It doesn't matter. That's what Mom would say. *It doesn't matter.* What does matter are the houses and what's in them.

"Nothing," I say. "I'll do it." I have to. All I've ever known is taking things and moving on. And so when I see Mrs. Donaldson the next afternoon, walk into her house with the rest of the maids, I'm not surprised when she doesn't notice me. I stood two feet away from her just days ago and shook her hand, but then I fit in, wasn't standing holding a bag of cleaning supplies and a vacuum. It's just like Mom says. People only see what they want to.

17

Joan and I have to clean the second floor (the Donaldsons, like a lot of rich people with huge old houses, don't use the third) and when we get there we go our separate ways. Shelly and Maggie clean together, but Joan has made it real clear that she does her thing and I do mine. It's fine with me and I head through the rooms Joan told me to do, dust and disinfect and vacuum. I also check for alarm sensors.

There's one sensor in the master bedroom, in a closet by what I can only describe as the most obvious safe ever, and that's it. I go downstairs and ask Maggie if she has an extra container of bathroom cleaner in order to check the windows. All of them, every single window and all of the outside doors I pass, have sensors. There's even one on a tiny decorative window high up on the kitchen wall. This is not a house Mom and I could easily get into without an in, that's for sure. But then we have one. Me.

I go back upstairs and turn on the vacuum. I push it around the floor, thinking about the silver. Getting it shouldn't be a problem. Stu's too cheap to buy supply bags, and so everyone has to buy one of those generic black duffels they sell at discount stores. I bought two, and the second one is still wrapped in the plastic it came in. It'll be easy to stick it into my regular bag and bring with me.

The only problem I can think of might be noise; silver clattering together definitely sounds different from jars of cleaning solution, but silver, good silver, is usually stored well wrapped. Another problem solved.

Getting it out of the house definitely won't be a problem. In the two days (it feels more like twenty) I've been Stu's poorly paid wage slave, four maids from different crews have just up and quit, three of them walking out in the middle of cleaning a house. That's the beauty of shitty jobs. No one expects you to stick around, and so when you leave no one thinks anything of it. By the time someone notices the silver is gone and the police get around to checking who was in the house and all that stuff, I'll be a blur in everyone's mind, "what's-her-name who quit."

However, all the sensors mean good security, and that means there might be a surveillance camera set up somewhere. I go back downstairs to find the security control panel so I can check. It's not by the front door and I head toward the back of the house. Maggie and Shelly are cleaning and I move past them quietly, slip into the dining room, and look around for the silver. It was in here the other day but I don't see it now. Damn. I'll have to look for that too.

The security panel is in a walk-in pantry right off the kitchen, and the Donaldsons have themselves a pretty good system. It's got a battery backup in case the power goes out or is cut, which is something most people don't bother with, never mind that cutting the power to someone's house isn't that hard. But there's no camera, and that's excellent news.

Now I just have to find the silver. I head back into the kitchen. All the drawers and cabinets hold brand-new-looking appliances and ordinary flatware. Now what? I look around to make sure no one is watching and make another slow circuit through the dining room.

Still nothing. If it's not here or in the kitchen, where can it be? I have to find it fast. Shelly and Maggie will be done soon, plus I still have one room to clean upstairs. At least I didn't get stuck with the downstairs. Dusting that walk-in pantry would be a pain in the ass and—

That's it. The pantry.

The silver is there. I can tell because I recognize the shape of the boxes on the top shelf. I lean against the wall, relieved, and then pull one box down and look in it just to make sure.

I'm right, and the silver is wrapped in pouches, just like I thought. I pull out a piece—it turns out to be a fork—and look at it. Early nineteenth century, definitely made before 1840. Engraving of some kind at the bottom, maybe a family crest. Very nice. I look a little closer at the engraving. It looks like some sort of bird. I turn the fork, trying to figure out exactly what the crest is.

"It's an eagle. I know it doesn't look like one, but it is. Or at least that's what my mother says. Isn't it ugly?"

Allison. Damn! I almost drop the fork but manage to shove it into the box and back on the shelf.

"I'm really sorry," I mutter, careful to stay turned away from her. "I was dusting when the box fell off the shelf. I promise it won't happen again."

"Don't worry about it. You should probably be on a stool or something so you don't hurt your back reaching that high. Do you want me to get you one? I think there's—"

"No, it's fine. I'm done in here anyway," I mumble, then duck my head and walk quickly by her.

I go back upstairs, careful not to move too fast, to act like everything is fine, and start dusting the last room Joan told me to clean. That was close, too close. What if she'd recognized me? I suppose then I wouldn't have to worry about her talking to me anymore—I'd be just a maid and like Mom said, girls like her don't notice maids.

But she did. She didn't know who I was but she acted just like she has every time I've seen her. She talked way too much. She was nice. She even offered to get me a stool. And I'm going to steal—it doesn't matter. She said the silver was ugly, plus her family has money, won't go broke because it's gone.

Telling myself this doesn't make me feel much better.

I sigh and glance around, wonder if anyone will be able to tell if I don't vacuum the room, and then realize Allison is standing in the doorway.

"So were you gonna say hello?" she says.

"Hey," I say cautiously. "You saw me . . ."

"When you came in. I saw you get out of the car. Did you see me?"

I shake my head. Oh, this is so bad.

"I didn't think so. I waved, but you didn't wave back. I would have come to say 'hey' sooner but I had to listen to my mother discuss her stupid party and then I ran into someone in the kitchen who'd just had a bunch of silver fall on her head."

Oh, this is so beyond bad.

"I'm sorry about that, by the way," she continues. "I mean, there I am blabbering away, and I'm such a loser because I didn't even realize it was you until you were walking away and then I was like, oh my God, that's Sydney!"

Okay, this is fixable. I just have to say the right thing. I can do this. "Look, I know you must be mad about me being . . ." I point at my uniform.

"What, a maid?" She gives me a look. "Why would I care about that? Is that why you didn't say anything to me?"

"Well . . ."

She rolls her eyes. "Silly. Is your head okay? Do you need some ice?"

"I'm fine." She doesn't really know why I didn't say anything to her. She thinks I'm embarrassed about being a maid, that I was clumsy and dropped silver on myself and that's it. Nothing more. She believes me. She doesn't look at me and see—she doesn't see what I am.

"So what have you been up to?" she asks.

"What?"

"You totally ran out of here the other night and I haven't seen you since. So I'm just wondering why you left, what you've been up to. You know, friend-catching-up type stuff."

"I . . . I guess I got kinda freaked out about everything, with me having this job and all," I tell her, which is sort of the truth because right now I am totally freaked. I mean, first she sees me as I'm checking out the silver, and then she believes my lame story. And now, in spite of the uniform, in spite of everything Mom has always said, she's still standing here wanting to talk to me. She's saying we're friends. The only people who've ever said they were my friends before were cops who'd try to butter me up to get me to rat on Mom. "You didn't—did you tell your mom I'm working here?"

She shakes her head. "She's kind of like—well, you know how some people just assume things about other people? My mom is like that. Actually my whole family is like that. It's embarrassing. Besides, she's totally obsessed with this party and wouldn't hear me if I said I was going to light myself on fire."

Okay, everything seems fine. I should tell her I need to get back to work, stop talking because Mom and I don't need any more information from her, but instead I find myself saying, "How's Brad?"

She grins at me. "Yesterday I went back to the little market. You know the one I saw you at that day? And he was there! I was"—she holds one hand out and wiggles it—"shaking just like this, and totally forgot everything I was going to say. So we're just standing there and we've already said hi and I'm like, now what? And then . . . I don't know how I did it, but I told myself okay, I have to do this, and so I asked him if he wanted to go out sometime. And do you know what he said?"

"Hmmm . . . yes?"

She laughs. "Yes! I still can't believe it. We went out to dinner last night and . . ." She spins around in a circle. "It was amazing. He's amazing."

"Are you going to see him today?"

"I hope so. He's calling later. What about you? What have you been doing?"

I shake my duster at her. "Nothing interesting."

"Oh, please. I know everyone around here, and they're all freaks. You've totally seen tons of stuff in their houses, and you've got to share details. All of them!"

"Well," I say, and end up telling her about the Walker house, and how Mr. and Mrs. Walker have separate everything. Which they keep locked. They even have two fridges, both of which have huge pad-locks on them.

"I knew it," Allison says, laughing. "They never go anywhere together. Like, if there's a party or some-thing, one of them shows up first and then the other one shows up like ten minutes later. But they always act like everything's fine. It totally proves people around here are so fake. That's why I like Brad. He's just—he's so real. You know? Like you, Sydney."

She grins at me. "Even if you have a name tag on that says you're Rebecca."

"Rebecca's my middle name," I say immediately, habit, and then feel like crap because I can tell Allison means what she said about me and she's wrong. "I figure it sounds more maidlike, don't you? And hey, I'm really glad about you and Brad." I know I've been lying nonstop but I really mean that last part.

"Rebecca!" Joan bellows, and from how loud she's yelling, she's clearly desperate for a nicotine fix. "Grab your stuff and let's go already!"

"I gotta go," I tell Allison.

"We have to hang out soon, okay?"

"Sure," I tell her. That I don't really mean. I can't mean it. She smiles at me and I wish that I could. I wish I could be her friend, a real friend. But I can't.

18

The next day is brutal. I spend a couple hours cleaning up puke at our second house—sick kids, I'm told, as if that makes some sort of difference. Then, at our third house, as I'm scrubbing a bathroom that belongs to a small boy who's being potty trained, Joan comes in and says, "Don't go in the master bedroom," before stomping off to smoke.

After I finish Little Mr. Pee-a-Lot's bathroom, I go out in the hallway to vacuum and a strong smell makes my eyes start to water and my lungs start to hurt. What has Joan done? I go outside and find her. She says, "Mixed ammonia and some other cleaner by mistake," and then offers me a cigarette, as if that will make my lungs hurt less.

I'm pretty sure things can't get much worse after that, but then we stop at our last house of the day.

It's a small one, a little cottage tucked on a side street at the very edge of Heaven. Maggie and Shelly moan as we park the car, and Joan says, "I keep hoping the damn place will burn down." I don't get what the big deal is—after spending all day in houses the size of small countries, how hard could it be to clean a normal-size house?

Very hard, as it turns out, because the owner, who is on the phone with Stu when we walk in, yelling that we're late, follows us everywhere. We're not allowed to split into our cleaning groups, and all four of us have to clean each room.

And the owner, who looks like a sweet grandmother, is actually demon spawn because not only does she follow us, she makes us clean everything over and over again. In one room, I dust a ceramic dog twelve times before she is satisfied. I also lose my name tag, but don't mention it because I have a feeling she'd make me stay until I found it, even if it took all night.

"God, I hate that house," Maggie says afterward, putting her feet up on the dashboard. Joan, who is busy lighting one cigarette off another one, nods, and swats at Maggie's feet. In the backseat, Shelly rubs her stomach and stretches out, knocking my cleaning duffel into my legs.

"Can you move over a little?" she asks. "I've hardly got room to breathe."

I grit my teeth and wedge myself closer to the door.

After we've gotten our assignments for tomorrow, I tell Stu I need a new name tag and listen to him yell, then get Joan to drive me to the strip mall where Mom said she'd leave the car. I can't drive to work—it wouldn't be a good idea for me to be connected to the car—and so Mom drives me to the edge of Heaven every morning and I walk to Stu's office, then have Joan drop me off someplace where Mom can either leave the car or come get me.

The car isn't there. I don't tell Joan that, of course, just say, "See you tomorrow!" and get a grunt and a puff of smoke blown in my face in return. This crappy-ass "job" I'm stuck with can't end soon enough. I dig out my cell and call Mom.

"Oh no," she says as soon as she hears my voice. "I totally forgot! Don't be mad, but I'm using the car right now. I'm on my way to meet Harold."

"So call and tell him you'll be late. My feet are killing me."

"Tonight is very important, baby. Just get a cab, okay?"

"Mom—"

"Oh, there he is. I gotta go. Cross your fingers for me!" She hangs up. I've got exactly three dollars on me. Great. That'll get me a cab ride to nowhere. I guess I'll have to walk.

I thought Mom would have dumped Harold by now, but she hasn't. I'm starting to think she's got other plans in mind, especially since she told me this morning that Harold keeps telling her about some huge place in Florida he's "watching" for friends who are in Tuscany for a year.

"All I have to do is listen to him talk about it, and how he'd love to take me there, and before you know it, I'll know exactly what kind of security the house has," she'd said. "Stuff like this falls into your lap for a reason, you know?"

"I know," I'd said, because it was too early to argue and because I noticed she was taking cough medicine without me nagging her to.

I walk into the shopping center's one restaurant, a pizza place. By the time I get home there's no way I'm going to want to do anything but sleep so I'll just eat now, have a couple of slices of pizza—no, not for three bucks. I guess I'll have a slice of pizza and then start walking. This really has been a crappy day.

The pizza place is deserted, but the gum-chewing girl working behind the counter tells me it'll take half an hour for a slice of cheese pizza.

"Half an hour?"

She snaps her gum between her teeth and stares at me like I'm stupid. I sigh and go outside to wait, lean against the wall and look out at the street. I guess it must be what passes for rush hour around here, as there's actually more than one car on the road. I start watching them. Car, truck, car, van, car, car, truck, car—car stopping suddenly and turning in to the parking lot. A station wagon. Greg's station wagon. I am suddenly really glad West Hill is a small town, the kind of town where you can't help but bump into people.

But he's a cop. I have to remember that.

"I thought that was you," Greg says when he gets out of the car. He's wearing a baseball cap that has a police logo on it. "What are you doing here?"

I point at the pizza place. "Half hour wait for a lousy slice of pizza."

"Is that what they said?"

I nod.

"Then it'll probably be more like an hour. They've been having problems with their oven."

"Great. Nice hat, by the way." Makes it very easy for me to remember he's a cop. Or should.

He leans against the wall next to me. "Funny how we keep running into each other."

"I wouldn't call me standing here minding my own business and you stopping to bother me running into each other."

He laughs. "I should have known you'd say that. So, what's wrong with my hat?"

"I said it was nice."

"I have an extra one in the car if you want it."

I look over at him, and he's grinning at me. Grinning at me and he took me to Edge Island because he wanted to, because he wanted to spend time with me, but he's a cop wearing a stupid hat with a cop logo on it, and all I want is one lousy slice of pizza and for Mom to actually think about something other than stealing and plans for stealing for five minutes and —I look away, stare back out at the road.

"Bad day?"

"Sort of," I say, glancing at him. He nods—I realize he has a few freckles on his nose (and I thought he couldn't get cuter)—and then takes his hat off. His hair is almost totally gone, cut so close that all that's left is pale fuzz.

"What happened?" I ask before I can stop myself.

"I had to get a haircut."

"Why?" Stupid question. How many cops have I met over the years trying out the "shaved-head badass" look? "Never mind. Cop thing, right?"

"Yeah. My shift sergeant told me to go to his barber and ask for the special. So I do, and this is what I get. Everyone thinks it's hysterical. You should have heard Ruthie. And, just so you know, feel free to jump in with 'oh, it's not that bad' anytime now."

I look over at him. I miss the crazy mess it was before. It suited him better somehow. "You look like more of a cop now."

"I look like a gnome."

"A gnome?"

He points at his ears.

"They look like ears to me."

"Really? Is that a compliment?"

"If you think me telling you your ears look like

ears is a compliment, then sure."

He laughs. "I had a nice time the other day."

I stare at him.

"What? I did. You should be a cop, you know that?"

I laugh. Weakly. "Oh yeah. It would be perfect for me."

"You've got the stare for it."

"That's just from years of watching—" I catch myself at the last second. Why can't I remember to think before I talk when I'm around him? "Watching cop shows. So it'll really be more than half an hour for a lousy piece of pizza?"

"Yeah. There's a place up the road that's not too bad as long as you order a sandwich. I was on my way there to grab something when I—well, you know. Saw you. You wanna go?"

"No." Yes.

He blushes, looks embarrassed and sad, and I hastily add, "I mean, I can't." It's true. I can't. I really can't. Mom would maybe forgive me the trip to Edge Island if I told her—maybe—but going out with a cop a second time? She'd kill me.

"Oh. I guess you're waiting for a ride to a costume

party fund-raiser or something?"

"What?"

He motions at my uniform.

"Right, this is my party dress. Who doesn't love bright yellow polyester?"

"Well, the only guy I know who does is Stu, but—"

"Yeah, the color-blind jackass. I can't believe I have to pay for this thing out of the crap he pays."

"You're working for him?"

"What gave it away? The uniform or the uniform?"

"Actually, I never would have guessed. I really thought you were waiting for a ride to another yacht club party. I mean, people who hang out there don't usually work, you know?"

Oh hell, I walked right into that.

"Yeah." I laugh, or at least fake something close to it. Right now if I could kick my own ass, I would. "Look, I crashed that party. I thought it would be fun. You know, I scrub their toilets so I figure . . ." Best to cut my losses and get out of here before I screw up more. "Anyway, I'm gonna go. Long walk home and all that."

"I can drive you."

"That's okay. It's really not very far." And I really

can't have him drive me home.

"Seriously," he says, and puts a hand on my arm. "You look tired and I'd . . . I'd really like to."

"Okay." I mean to say no, I do, but I'm really tired and my brain is probably still a little scrambled from Joan's cleaner-fume creation earlier. Plus his hand is warm on my arm and I just . . . I like being with him.

In the car, he runs a hand over his head and sighs. I guess he misses his hair. I miss it too.

"You really got a shitty haircut," I tell him.

I figure that should get me thinking properly (and not about things like his hair, or him) and maybe even get me kicked out of the car, but instead he laughs as he pulls out onto the road and says, "Yeah, I know. So, what have you been up to?"

"Nothing much." There's a piece of paper sticking out of the glove compartment. It takes me a second to realize what it is, but it's the receipt for the ferry tickets. I wonder why he kept it. I mean, it's a strange thing to hold on to.

I flick the receipt with one finger. "Is this whole ride home thing a ploy to make me pay for my ticket from the other day?"

He laughs. "Are you insane? No, never mind, don't answer that. It's just . . . I don't know. I wanted to keep it. The whole day was . . . good. Special."

"Really?"

"Yeah. That okay?"

Yes. It's more than okay. It's amazing. I like him, and I think he actually likes me. Really likes me.

But he's a cop, and I can't do this. I have to stop this . . . whatever with him. For real, this time.

"It's fine. But I—look, just drop me off here."

"You live at"—he squints at the road sign we're passing—"mile marker forty-six? Behind the sign or in front of it?"

"Just pull over, will you?"

"Dani—"

"Pull over," I tell him again, almost shouting, trying to sound angry because this really can't go on, it can't, and start to open my car door.

He looks over at me, eyes wide, and does.

"Don't follow me or anything like that," I say, and start to get out of the car.

"Look," he says, just as I'm about to slam the door. "I'm not—I get that you don't want to go out with me, okay? I didn't mean to make you feel like you have to get out of the car on the side of the road to get away from me. I'm sorry."

I stare at him. "You—?"

"I really am sorry," he says again. He looks miserable. He had a good time with me when we went to Edge Island. He thought it was special, and now he thinks I don't want to be around him.

This is the end of whatever is going on between us, or will be as soon as I walk away. I know that, just like I know I should be proud of myself, or happy, or something like it. But I'm not. I feel as miserable as he looks.

"You don't have to apologize, okay?"

Now it's his turn to stare. A car drives by, honking at us for not being far enough off the road. "Why not?"

"Because you don't."

"So you're getting out of the car on the side of the road because why?"

"Just . . . just because, okay?"

He grins at me, wide and sunny and sweet in a way I didn't know grins could be. "You are absolutely the most logical person I've ever met."

"Oh, shut up." I start walking away from him, heading down the road.

"No, seriously," he says, driving along next to me, window rolled down. "Is it just that you don't like questions or you don't like me?"

I look over at him. I know I should say, "You," but he's looking at me, those green eyes intent on my face, and there's something in them I can't read, that I don't recognize but that makes my breath catch.

"Questions," I say.

"Okay, I won't ask any more. Now can I please drive you home?"

I stop walking. I still can't read the look in his eyes but I like it. It makes me feel—I don't know. Safe, somehow. Which is stupid, because I'm not safe with him.

I know that. I do, really, but I get in the car anyway. And when he smiles at me and says, "Now, this isn't a question, but if I was going to listen to music, would you have any preferences?" I smile back.

19

When the house comes into view I figure his reaction will be like Mom's. I mean, I can see that the house is small and dark, built so it's all sharp angles. You can't not see it. I think I love it because it's like that. It's what it is and you can't cover it up.

He stops the car and doesn't say anything.

I look over at him after a minute. "Don't like the house, right?"

"Actually, I do. And it seems . . . it seems completely perfect for you. You must love it."

"I do," I say, surprised. "Mom can't stand it, but I think it's great. The side of the house facing the water is almost all windows and in the morning, when the sun rises . . . it's amazing. I could live here forever so easily but— " I break off, aware I'm babbling. Why is it that I don't talk about any of this stuff with Mom, who wouldn't really listen but at least isn't a cop?

"How about sunsets?"

"What?"

"You know, when the sun sets. They must look pretty amazing too."

"I haven't really noticed. Mostly I just get home from work, make dinner, and then pretend I'm going to clean up and fall asleep on the sofa."

"I could make you dinner."

I look over at him. He's fidgeting with the steering wheel. "I mean, if you wanted. Just as friends, I swear."

"You want to make me dinner?"

"Well, I thought I did. But now with the questions starting again . . . " He grins at me. "Yeah, I do. And okay, I also want to see this great view you keep talking about too."

No one's ever cooked for me. Mom sometimes brings food home and once she hooked up with a chef who made eggs in the morning before she kicked him out. Or maybe it was waffles. I don't really remember. It was a long time ago.

"Okay," I tell him. And so it ends up that not only

does he drive me home, I willingly take him inside.

He likes all the things in the house I do: the furniture, the pictures the owners left behind, and he spends a couple of minutes staring out the living room windows.

"Wow," he says. "It is an amazing view."

I thought it would be weird having him here, but it doesn't feel weird. It feels nice. I'm having . . . I'm having fun.

"Oh, hey, the kitchen's got a nice view too," he says, walking in there. "I can look at the—oh. Pile of rocks—while I cook. Okay, what's the deal with the rocks?" He points out the kitchen window.

"I know," I say. The owners have some weird stone formation on the front lawn. "When Mom signed the lease, one of the things on there was that we had to promise not to disturb the . . . whatever it is."

"So they make one side of the house all glass and then pile up stones to block the view? You know what? People are weird."

"Look who's talking."

He laughs. "Yeah, and right back at you." He starts opening cabinets and pulling out stuff. "Okay, what have we got here?"

"You know, you don't really have to make any-thing. There's peanut butter and bread and I nor-mally—"

"Hey, I can cook."

"I'm sure you can. It's just—"

"Believe me, between my mom and my brothers, I had to learn. My mom can't cook and my brothers are totally worthless in the kitchen. My dad always did the cooking. I used to help out sometimes and then after he . . . after he died, I just ended up doing all of it."

"Brothers?"

"Yep. Two of 'em. One older, one younger. Do you have a colander?"

"No."

"That's all right." He grins at me. "I'll improvise. You want me to call you when I'm done?"

I shake my head.

"Oh, okay. Want to watch a master in action, huh?"

I laugh. He grins at me again. "I should have known. Afraid I'm going to poison you, right?"

"No. I just want to watch. No one's ever—no one's ever made me dinner. It's . . . I don't know. Nice."

"Yeah?"

"Yeah."

"You really do have a pretty smile," he says, and then turns away, starts opening cans and turning on the stove. I watch him work, nervous and happy and all mixed up inside.

He makes spaghetti and serves it with green beans and garlic bread.

"You're a miracle worker," I tell him as I start on my third piece of bread. "Seriously. I know I saw you do it and all, but still."

He laughs. "You're a lot nicer about my cooking than my ex-girlfriend."

"You had a girlfriend?"

"Thanks. Really, that did so much for my ego."

"No one should dump anyone who can make something like this. Hell, even though you're a cop, I think my mother might . . ." See? Why do I do this around him?

"Well, it was more than my cooking. She wanted to get married and I . . ." He shrugs.

"She wanted to marry you?"

"Again with the ego bruising. But yeah, she did. Or said she did. I don't think she really wanted to, but we'd been going out since high school and it was like—it was like all we'd known was each other. I think she knew trying to push us into something more would be what we both needed to move on. Plus, she said my spaghetti sauce sucked. How about you?"

"How about me what?"

"Oh, right. Questions. Sorry. Here, take this last piece of bread."

I do. God, it's good. "Okay, you can ask me a question."

"Really? Wait, don't count that. Hmmm. I know. Did you go to high school around here?"

"No."

"I didn't think so. I would have remembered you." He grins at me. "So where did you go?"

"No, I mean I didn't—I never went."

"Never?"

I shrug. "Nope. Sometimes I wish I'd had the chance to go, but Mom always said she could teach me more than—" I break off. "I was . . . home-schooled, I guess you could say. What about you? Are you in college or anything?"

"Not really. I mean, I take classes when I can, but at

the rate I'm going I'll be a hundred before I'm done."

"They have cop college degrees?"

He laughs. "Sort of. I could get a criminal justice degree or something, but I'm taking social work classes. See, after my dad and . . . everything, Mom sent me to see this social worker friend of hers. A counselor. I was really pissed about going at first but she was—she helped me. So I figure if I can help someone like that, I'd like to."

He clears his throat. "How about you?"

"How about me what? College?"

He nods.

"I can't go to college. Not with everything—I didn't even go to high school."

"So? You could get your GED."

"And then go to college?"

"Sure, why not?" The way he says it, like it could be so easy, makes me think for a crazy second that I could. And then I remember who I am.

"Because."

"Oh, okay. Great reason."

"Look, I'd like to go. I mean . . ." I trail off. I would like to go. But it will never happen. "Right now things are—I have to work."

"I get that. What did you do before you started working for Stu?"

Well, recently I was with my mom in Pennsylvania, where we spent a couple of days getting ready to rob a house. We did, and then we came here. "You know, crap job kind of stuff. And now there's Stu and—" I gesture at my uniform. "I think this thing would glow in the dark."

He laughs. "How about your mom? What does she do?"

I get up and start taking dishes over to the sink.

"All right," he says, getting up and bringing the rest of them over. "I get it. Over the question limit, right?"

"What does your mom do?"

He grins at me. "You're really good at answering questions with questions, you know that? She's a teacher. Middle school, earth science. You ever want to know anything about rocks, I'm the person to ask."

"Really?" I grin back, take the dish he's holding, and put it in the dishwasher. "So if, say, I wanted to know—" My cell rings, startling me. "Hold on a second. Hello?"

"Baby, do you still need a ride?" Mom's voice, brittle and very tense. Things with Harold must not be going well.

"No, I'm home already."

"Do me a favor and make some coffee, will you? I'll be there in a little while."

"Okay," I say, and she hangs up. She wants coffee. Home early and wanting coffee means things with Harold went beyond bad, and she's going to be in a horrible mood because of it.

"You've got to go," I tell him. "That was my mom on the phone and . . ." I take the plate he's loading into the dishwasher out of his hands, motion him toward the door. "Look, I'll finish that."

"I don't mind."

"No, it's not that, it's—look." I take a deep breath. "Thank you for dinner."

"Wow, you must really want me out of here." He's still grinning but it seems forced and there's something strange in his gaze.

I open the front door, and he leaves without saying anything, not even good-bye.

What if he's mad? I can't let him leave mad because

I . . . because he's a cop.

"Look," I say, and head outside, catch up to him. "My mom"—hates cops, would kill me for having one in the house—"she's strict. But I—thank you for making me dinner. Really. I had fun."

He looks at me and I realize what the something in his eyes was. It was hurt. I realize that because I see it fade, watch him smile at me for real, a smile that lights up his face.

"Me too," he says, leaning in toward me, and I can't move, can only stare at him, startled. He brushes a thumb across my cheek, a nothing touch, but the look in his eyes is so serious, so—so not a way anyone has ever looked at me.

When he goes, I watch him drive away.

20

Things with Mom and Harold aren't that bad after all. Mom came home in a horrible mood, but that's because she had to get mad at Harold during dinner. She could tell he was getting ready to pull a "you seem too good to be true" speech—with three marriages come and gone, he's a little gun-shy when it comes to women.

Anyway, it pissed her off because she says, "I thought he was stupider than that, baby. And so now I have to be extra careful with him. It's annoying."

After I make her a couple of cups of coffee she calms down and leaves a fake tearful message on Harold's voice mail saying she loves him and wants him but things are complicated and maybe they need a break. He calls back later that night, but Mom doesn't answer. She listens to the message he leaves, though.

"Nothing like shaking them up," she says as she turns her phone off, smiling at me. "Tell them you love them and then run away—makes them crazy. I bet you I've got the security code for the alarm system at the house down in Florida by the end of next week."

"Maybe we won't be here next week. I mean, after I go back to the Donaldson house we won't need to hang around."

"We'll see."

I know what that means. I'm not happy about it, but what can I do? Once Mom decides she wants something, there's no stopping her. "I'm going to bed. I have to spend all day tomorrow cleaning up people's crap. And I do mean crap."

She looks at me. "It's what you have to do. And if you get the Donaldson house, you—"

"I know, I'll call."

"Good."

In the morning Mom is so tired that she actually stops on our way out to the car. At first I think she's checking her cell for messages, because she's looking at it, but then I realize that she's just standing there.

"Mom?"

"I'm coming. I think that stupid fish Harold insisted I try was bad. I feel like shit."

"Make sure you take it out on him when he calls, then."

She grins at me. "Good one, baby. Feel like breakfast?"

I roll my eyes at her. "Fine, we can stop on the way and get you, I mean me, a donut."

Work is the same as always—long, boring, and filled with Joan nagging us for gas money—but when we get back to the office at the end of the day Allison is waiting outside, sitting on the decorative bench Stu has warned us to never sit on. It's okay for there to be maids in Heaven but we're not supposed to actually be seen. She waves when we pull in.

"Isn't that the Donaldsons' daughter?" Maggie asks. "What's she doing here?"

"Who cares?" Joan says, but looks at me in the rearview mirror. "I think she's waving at you. What did you do, steal something from her?"

I laugh and after a second Shelly joins in—she's one of those people who hates to think she's missing a joke. Joan gives me another look, then shrugs and lights a cigarette.

I say hi to Allison when we're on our way inside, very aware that everyone is watching us, even Joan (though she's mostly trying to suck down as much smoke as possible before she goes inside).

"Hey," Allison says. "I was going to call you but then I realized I don't have your last name so I couldn't get your number. So then I figured I'd . . ."

"So you came here. Look, I'd love to hang out but I'm still at work and we've got this meeting . . ."

"I can totally wait." Allison smiles at Maggie and Shelly, who finally stop gawking and go inside. "I've been dying to talk to you! We have to go eat ice cream or something completely fattening because my mom is obsessed with losing, like, a pound before the party and so there's nothing to eat but some disgusting things that look like candy bars but so aren't and plus —" She leans over and grabs my arm. "Brad! We're dating! Like, for real! Oh my God, I've finally said it out loud."

I should be alarmed that she's tracked me down, but I'm not. It's nice someone wants to hang out with me. I just wish I could.

"It might be a while. We usually get a lecture on

some exciting new cleaning product before we're allowed to go and—"

"I don't mind waiting. There's some stuff—" She breaks off, looking a little unsure, and I wonder what she means. I don't get a chance to ask, though, because Stu comes out and clears his throat, my cue to go inside. I do, turning my cell off as I sit next to Joan and listen to him outline an exciting new way to clean toilets—like that's even possible.

When he's finally done, I go meet Allison.

It's not a big deal, seeing her. Not really. After all, I know what I'm doing.

I think.

Allison and I get floats at the ice cream place. I notice people looking at my uniform—the tourists kind of curiously, the rich summer people with eyes that go vacant as soon as they see it—and I figure Allison will probably be embarrassed by it, be embarrassed by me. But she doesn't seem to care at all and even introduces me to everyone who stops and says hi to her.

"I think you're freaking people out," I tell her after I've just shaken hands with a horrified-looking man dressed in a polo shirt with the collar turned up.

If you ask me, I'm the one who should have looked horrified.

"Please. Everyone around here has such sticks up their asses. Besides, did you see what he was wearing? He should be thanking us for talking to him."

I laugh. "That's what I was thinking."

We talk for a while more and even though I know Mom is waiting for me I'm not in a hurry to leave. It's nice, just sitting around talking to Allison, and for a while I'm able to pretend we're friends, real friends. She tells me about going to the beach with Brad. I tell her about cleaning the crazy demon spawn lady's house.

"I guess you must be totally ready to go back to school then, right?" Allison asks.

"Pretty much." And just like that, all the fun I was having totally disappears. I can't pretend I'm just sitting here talking to a friend anymore. I'm not a college student, never will be. And Allison—I'm not her friend. She doesn't know my last name. She doesn't even know my real name.

"Look, I should—" I say, and then break off because she looks nervous like she did before. "What's wrong?"

"Well, it's just . . . okay. I'm glad I'm going to school, but Brad is—I really like him, you know? I don't want the summer to end. And then I find out . . ." She pauses, looks down at her cup. "You know how he was acting weird for a while? I knew—well, I thought James might have said something to him."

"Why?" I'm sure he said something. James reminds me of Mom in a lot of ways, and she would have said something.

She turns her cup around in her hands. "It's just how he is. And then, yesterday, Brad told me he and James ended up at the same party a couple of days after we got here and James told him I didn't really like him, that I thought it was funny to have some beach guy chasing after me."

"Maybe he was joking. Brother-type stuff, you know?"

"Yeah," she says slowly, and I can tell we both know it wasn't a joke at all. "Maybe."

"So," Mom says that night, after she's done giving me the silent treatment. "What's going on with you?"

I'm lying on the sofa trying to sleep but when I hear her voice I rub my eyes and sit up. I knew what was coming the moment I got in the car and she didn't say a word about how late I was, but I also knew I'd have to wait. Mom does things her own way and in her own time. She always has.

"Stu wouldn't shut up about some new grout cleaner. And no, I haven't seen the schedule, so I don't know when we'll do the Donaldson house again. But as soon as I do—"

"Baby, I'm not talking about the house. What I mean is, what's going on with you?" Mom sits down, curling an arm around my shoulders. "I know you wouldn't be over an hour late because some moron was talking about cleaner. I know there's someone. You want to tell me about him?"

Tell Mom about Greg? I can't do that. And besides, it's not like we're . . . anything, really. He just took me out. And made me dinner. And is a cop. No, I definitely can't mention him. She'd be furious.

She wouldn't get the Allison thing either. I know how she feels about people in general, and the whole idea of friends in particular. She thinks people are there to use and nothing more.

"Well, the thing is . . . the Donaldsons have a son, and I figured any information is good information, right?"

I can't believe I just said that. She'll never buy it.

But she does, because she says, "James, right?" She doesn't even sound surprised. I can't believe that either. She thinks I would have anything to do with him? He's everything I can't stand in guys. He's someone who charms and lies and then walks away. He's—

He's everything I'm supposed to be.

"I saw you together at the party," she says. "Not that hard to figure out, baby. He's not the kind of face you forget. How long have you been seeing him?"

"I . . . um. Not long. And I know you're probably mad, so I'll stop—"

"I'm glad," she says, and I stare at her, stunned. If I was messing around with James she'd be happy?

"Don't look so surprised, baby. Remember, I did see you two together. And look, I know what happened with—oh, what's his name?—never mind, it doesn't matter. It was ages ago. Anyway, I know it was—"

She squeezes my shoulder and I barely, just barely, manage not to flinch. "I know it was hard and I'm glad you're out there having a little fun now. It's what you should be doing. It's what makes life worth living. Plus, I know you'd never do anything stupid. We both know what really matters, and it's all that silver just waiting for us."

"But—" I say, and then fall silent because I can't say what's next. I can't say she's wrong. I can't say James is nothing to me and always will be. I can't tell Mom I don't care about the silver. I can't say I'm not like her and don't want to be. I can't say it because it would hurt her. I can't say it because it doesn't matter. Everything's set and there's no way out of it now.

21

I don't normally care what day it is but I know to-day is Thursday. Why? Because I have the day off. No scrubbing toilets, no vacuuming, no sitting in the car with Shelly pigging up every inch of space and Joan doing her part to keep the cigarette industry in business.

I get up and make eggs and bacon and coffee. Well, sort of. I don't know if I'd eat the eggs, but the bacon seems to have turned out okay. Mom's still asleep when I'm done, which is surprising because normally the minute she smells coffee she's up and asking when it will be ready.

I go to her bedroom. Her door is open and the blinds are up but she's lying in bed staring at the wall.

"Mom?"

"Hey, baby." She sounds awful, like there's a

whistling teakettle stuck in her chest.

"You sound awful."

"I just slept funny. Will you bring me a cup of coffee?"

"How about"—I go into the bathroom, look around until I find the bottle of cough syrup, and then go back out and wave it at her—"some of this?"

"I'm not coughing anymore," she says, and then does, twice.

"What?" she says when I look at her. "I told you I slept funny. Will you please bring me some coffee? I've got to meet Harold in—what time is it?"

I tell her and she hops out of bed, saying, "Coffee, baby, now. I've got to get ready."

She rushes into the bathroom, turns the shower on. I go downstairs and come back up with a mug. She sticks one arm out of the shower for it.

"Thank you," she says as I wrap her fingers around the mug. "I feel better already. Don't I sound better? I do. So stop making your worry face and go do something fun."

"How do you know what face I'm making? You can't even see me."

She laughs. "And now I know I'm right. Seriously,

baby, go out, have fun. Maybe go see that someone you've been—"

Eww. Must stop her now. "Okay, okay, I'll go out."

Her laughter follows me into the hall. I go back downstairs and clean up the kitchen. After she's left to meet Harold, pressing a kiss on my cheek before she heads off to meet her cab, I go into town, end up at the grocery store. I stand in the cough and cold remedy aisle again, looking for something she can take. Or rather, will take.

I skip the cough syrup—that certainly hasn't done much good—and check out the cold remedies. Most of them say they'll clear a stuffy head or nose but I don't see anything about fixing odd noises when you breathe. But maybe that's "stuffy chest."

"I'm starting to think this is your second home."

Greg. I know his voice. Strange but true, and not only that, I'm glad to hear it. I turn and he's standing a few feet away, smiling at me. He's wearing his uniform today. His nose is a little sunburned.

My first instinct is to—well, it should be to smile politely and leave. I know this. But my actual first instinct is to smile back. To smile and stay.

"Your mom still not better?"

I know I told him about Mom—and where I live and actually let him in the house and want to talk to him now, and oh crap, let's just not go there. I just have to stop screwing up around him. "What, now you're a doctor?"

"Yeah, asking about your mother means I'm a doctor. Have you ever been to a doctor? If I was one, I would have . . ." He picks a box off the shelf and holds it out toward me. When I take it, he says, "Okay, that'll be a hundred and eighty bucks."

"Hilarious." I put the box back on the shelf.

"Yes, I can see I've really cheered you up. What's going on?"

"Nothing. What are you doing here?" Why am I still talking to him?

"I just finished . . ." He gestures toward the front of the store.

"What? Guarding a dangerous vegetable shipment?"

He doesn't say anything, but his face turns a little red.

"Oh, please, tell me you weren't actually guarding vegetables." I manage, just barely, not to laugh, but I hear it in my voice.

His face is definitely red.

"You were!" I am laughing now.

"I should have known. The humiliation of my having to come down here and watch over a truck cheers you up. But just so you know, it wasn't vegetables. It was—" He grins at me. "A cake."

"A cake?" I start laughing even harder.

"Hey, I'll have you know it's a very special cake. It's for two hundred and fifty people and it's to celebrate the first town meeting." He pauses for a second and moves closer. "You want to know what the worst part is?"

"What?"

"They spelled West Hill wrong, made it all one word. When I pointed this out, you know what the bakery guy told me?"

I shake my head.

"'Oh, I'll just throw some sprinkles on and no one will notice.'"

We look at each other and both start laughing.

"Sorry," I say after a moment. "It's just that—"

"I spent my morning watching over a cake?"

"Yeah."

He grins at me. "Do you want to go get something

to eat? There's a New York System place just down the road."

I shouldn't. But I want to. "New York System?"

"Yeah."

"You do know this isn't New York, don't you?"

He laughs. "That's a yes, right?"

"Me pointing out you don't know what state you live in makes it a 'yes,' how?"

"'Cause you're still here," he says. "And you're smiling again."

I go to lunch with him. He says he would drive but he walked to the grocery store from the police station, and so before I know it he's in my car. The car Mom and I share. The car I know for a fact she sure doesn't want any cops to notice, much less ride in.

"This isn't what I expected," he says when we get in. "I thought it would be more—well, you."

"This is me. I'm a very . . ." I look at the steering wheel, hoping it will contain a clue as to what kind of car this is. I never really notice our cars because we never have them for very long. Great. No words, just a logo. "I'm a very midsize sedan kind of girl."

He laughs. "I can think of a million words to describe you, Dani, but a midsize sedan kind of girl? Not what springs to mind."

I look over at him, ready to ask what that means, and stop, the words drying up in my throat. He's looking at me and smiling and it's not like I haven't seen Greg smile or look at me before or anything. It's just . . . it's not even what he said. It's just the way he said it, like he really could think of a million words to describe me. Like he already knows them by heart.

Wow. I'm feeling—

"Uh, red light," Greg says, and I slam on the brakes.

Happy. I'm happy.

I'm so screwed.

It's all I can think about as the light turns green and we drive into the heart of West Hill, and I'm torn between wishing I'd never agreed to go to lunch with him and knowing that I'm really glad that I am. Which isn't so much being torn, I guess, as it is realizing that, for the first time in ages, I actually want to spend time with a guy.

"There it is," Greg says, pointing out the window. "My home away from home. I know you're thinking,

"'Wow, what a glamorous police station. How on earth can I get a tour?'"

I'm in a car with a guy who's a cop, and we just drove by a police station. The station where he works, and which reminds me all over again of exactly what I'm supposed to be doing—which is avoiding cops—and what I'm doing instead. And how I shouldn't be doing it.

And yet I am doing it—I am with him, and what's more, I'm happy I am—and that makes me mad. At him, but mostly at myself.

"You don't know what I'm thinking."

Okay, I might have overdone it there because Greg looks at me, eyebrows raised. But all he says is, "I know," and then, quietly, "You're not easy to figure out. It's one of the reasons why I like you."

So SO screwed.

"Here it is," he says, before I have time to think of a reply—not that I'm sure I could think of anything to say right now—and gestures at a door squeezed into a tiny space between two stores. "And hey, look, there's a parking space. Now that's what I call—well, okay. I call it you turning down this street and not stopping."

"I don't want the car to get scratched. Or dented."

And I sure don't want to leave it parked in broad daylight a block from the police station. Or let myself think about the fact that I'm still with him.

"Well, that's less likely to happen, especially since we're still driving. Should I just take a nap and have you wake me up when we get there?"

"We're like two blocks away. Your cake delivery supervising duties tire you out or something?"

"Two and a half blocks. Oh, wait, are you stopping now? Are you sure you want to? Look, there's a whole other empty block just waiting for you—"

"Don't tempt me." I pull the car into a parking space. "So what is this New York thing?"

"New York System," he says as we get out of the car.

"Yeah, that answers my question."

"You'll see," he says, and grins, bumping his shoulder against mine. I decide not to think about how screwed I am anymore.

Then I find out what New York System means.

A hot dog. It's a hot dog. We walk into the smallest and oldest-looking restaurant I've ever seen and that's all people are eating. And the place is packed too, standing room only like we're in a club or something. Greg joins what I'm guessing is the line and I stand behind him watching people eat these things, which appear to be nothing more than small hot dogs covered with chili.

"Okay," I ask him when we're almost about to order. "Why do you call chili dogs New York—?"

"Shhh," he whispers in pretend terror. "Don't say the c word. You'll get us thrown out of here."

I look at him. He's smiling and his hair is still nothing but pale fuzz and he's in his uniform (a cop, he's a cop) and he asks way too many questions and . . . and I'm still happy to be here.

"Chili," I whisper back, just to watch him laugh. Which he does, and then says, "Six" to the guy behind the counter.

"Six?" I ask. "Is this your only meal of the day or something?"

"Watch," he says, and I do, see the guy line up a row of hot dog buns on one arm. He adds the hot dogs next and then, in a strangely graceful way, dumps on mustard, onion, something from a big spice shaker, and then the not-chili. It takes him maybe ten seconds and he doesn't spill or drop anything.

"Wow." I look over at Greg, who's grabbed two sodas, grinning at me as he pretends to linger over the diet ones for a second, and then gets in line to pay.

I look at him and I'm—you know what? I'm tired of worrying, of thinking about what I should do. I'm just going to let things be, just for this one lunch.

"Hey, Dani, I think I see a place to sit," Greg says. I like the way he says my name, the name I've always wanted for the me I've never gotten to be.

"Yeah, yeah, I'm coming," I tell him, and watch him smile.

22

Greg finds us a spot in a corner. I'm not sure I'll be able to eat because the place is still so packed I can't move my arms—and because I'm not really fond of chili—but it turns out there's just enough space, and whatever is on the hot dogs doesn't taste like chili at all. It's a weird combination of meat sauce and gravy and it's good. Really good.

"So did that stuff you got for your mom before help at all?" Greg says when he hands me my second hot dog.

"I guess. She's fine now. Well, sort of."

"Sort of?"

"She says she's okay but she doesn't seem better. You know?"

"She should go to the doctor," Greg says, and picks up the last hot dog. Not-chili leaks onto his shirt cuff. He sighs. "The downside of the New York System."

"I haven't had that problem."

"I suppose that's true as long as I don't look at the floor."

"Hey!" I kick him lightly in the shin, and then realize I'm flirting. Actual honest-to-God flirting. It's fun. "And I've tried to get her to go to the doctor. She won't go."

"There's a clinic right outside town," he says. "The doctors there are pretty nice."

I shake my head. "It doesn't matter how nice they are. I don't remember her ever going to the doctor for anything. But I just . . . I don't know what to do." I bite my lip.

"Hey," he says, and leans over, brushes his thumb across my mouth. "You'll figure it out."

I nod, caught by that simple touch. By how good it feels. Being with him makes the whole world sharper somehow. More real. More everything.

"I should probably go." I should, I really should. Except I'm not getting up and walking away or even moving.

"Me too." He isn't moving either, and we just

stare at each other for the longest time. Then someone says, "Hello, waiting to sit down," and it breaks the tension because we both laugh.

Once we're outside, though, we both stand on the sidewalk. Out of the corner of my eye I can see our reflection in a store window. I can see how close we are. I can see him looking at me, a smile on his face. I smile at his reflection. His smile gets broader.

"What's so funny?" I ask.

"I—oh hell. Here goes. I was just thinking I've never wanted to go back to work less than I do right now and it's because you're here and you're looking at me. Only you aren't, really. You're looking at my reflection."

"I'm looking at you." I turn, face him. He grins more and in the bright sunshine I see the freckles on his nose, lurking under his sunburn. I see that when his hair grows out it'll be that strange mix of red and blond and brown again, something that shouldn't look right on anybody but will on him.

"Dani?" he says quietly, moving closer. He's going to kiss me, I know it. I am standing here and know it. A cop is going to kiss me. Greg is going to kiss me, and I want him to. I want him to kiss me.

Someone bumps into me then, hard, and I look up to see a middle-aged guy I don't know . . . and Mom.

"I'm so sorry," she says, "I wasn't watching my step." Her voice is polite, friendly even, but her eyes—she's furious. Really and truly furious in a way I've only seen her with others. Not with me. Never me.

"It's okay," I mumble, and watch her walk off arm in arm with the guy, who must be Harold. She doesn't turn back but I watch her steer Harold into a store and know she's hanging around to keep an eye on me, to see what I do next.

"I need to get home," I tell Greg, and take off before he can say anything. I think he calls out something as I'm crossing the street, but I'm too freaked out to listen.

She saw me. She saw me with Greg. She saw me almost kiss him. I race back to the car and drive home, where I wait and wait and wait some more.

She comes back what feels like a million years later. I'm sitting outside, waiting for her, and I watch her pay the cab driver and tell him very sweetly to have a nice afternoon. She walks toward the house, toward me, still all smiles. She stops when she's standing at the foot of the steps, and the smile is long gone from her face.

"I didn't think you were so stupid." Her voice is very quiet, almost a whisper. "Your whole life, Danielle, your whole life you know what cops do. What they've done to your father, to me, to us, and yet I see you today and . . ." She shakes her head, disgust on her face.

"Mom—"

She stretches one hand out, as if she's pushing my words away, and turns so she can't see me, looks out at the water. "I don't want to hear it. I just want to know how long it's been going on."

"There's nothing—" I break off because she's turned back to look at me and is calling me a liar without ever saying a word. She's saying it in the way her mouth turns down at the corners, in the flatness of her eyes. "I'm not—we're not like that."

"You're not sleeping with him?" Her voice is very sharp now.

"No! I was—" I look down at the ground. There's no way I can tell her all the stuff I should have before. Not now. "I was just talking to him. He was at the yacht club thing, and when I saw him today

I thought I'd see what he knows about the Donald-sons, about their security system. Just in case, you know? I was just—"

"If you say 'doing what you're supposed to,' I—" I look up at her. She's staring at me, and her hands are clenched into shaking fists by her sides. "Your father lied to me. He said everything would be fine, swore it would be forever, and then he was gone. He broke my heart, did it like it was nothing, left me alone, and . . ."

She shakes her head. "No one's doing that to me again, not ever, so you look at me and you tell me the truth. First, does he know about me?"

"Yes. But not who you are. Just—he knows I'm living here with my mom."

"Does he know where you work?"

I look down at the ground. "Yes."

"Where we live?"

"Yes," I mumble.

"Of all the—dammit, Danielle. What were you thinking? No, you know what? I don't even want to know. Maybe you've forgotten all those times we had to put up with people like him hauling me around, hauling you around, threatening us—"

"I haven't, I swear," I tell her, and my voice is cracking, my eyes burning. "I would never—"

"Never what? Screw things up for us? You look at me—" She squats down so we're face to face, her eyes looking directly into mine. "You look at me and you tell me this cop doesn't know why we're here. You—" She grabs my hands. "Tell me."

I yank my hands away. "What? You know I would never do that."

She doesn't say anything, just keeps looking at me.

"Mom, I owe you everything. You're the only one who's ever wanted me around, who—" I can hardly breathe. It feels like something inside me is broken. How can she think I would betray her like that?

"Shhhh," Mom says, her expression softening, her gaze no longer quite so angry, and sits down on the stairs next to me. "You're my girl, baby. That's never going to change. I just—you know how much mistakes can cost, don't you?"

I nod, wipe at my face, my still burning eyes. "I'm sorry."

"I know." She rests her head on my shoulder. "And it won't happen again. I know that too. I know that—" She coughs twice, and I feel her wince.

"Mom?"

"Not now, Danielle."

"But you—"

"I'm fine."

"You need to go to the doctor."

"What did I just say?" Mom says sharply. "We have other things to think about. Important things. Are you ready for them?"

"Y-Yes."

"What was that?"

"Yes. I'm ready. I swear I am."

"Good. Because I believe in—"

"I know. What you can hold in your hands, what you can sell."

"That's right," she says, and squeezes my hand. "But I believe in you and me too, baby. We've got it all figured out. We're winners."

"We are," I say, but I don't feel like one.

23

I'm tired on my way to work in the morning and Mom is quiet, drives with the radio off and her window rolled down, the wind whistling through the car and making it impossible for us to talk. I know she isn't mad with me anymore but I know Mom, and what she saw yesterday will stay with her. She will look at me differently for a while and I will be told even less than usual about where we're going, what we'll be doing. She won't do this to hurt me. She'll do it because it's just how things are. How she is.

"You'll call if you need to," she says when she stops the car.

"I will," I say, and five minutes after Stu has handed out the day's assignments, I do. When I'm done talking to her I toss my cell in the Dumpster. Stu has it emptied every morning—he reminds us of it whenever he's talking about planning and efficiency. He says it shows he's always on top of things. There's a lot of things I won't miss about this job. Stu is in the number-two spot.

On the way to our first house, Joan tells me I look tired. Actually, what she says is, "You look like shit. Don't think I'm picking up after your slack ass." You can guess which spot she holds in "things I won't miss about this job." I yawn, ignoring her, and watch Shelly rub her stomach. Maggie reads our list out loud. The Donaldson house is last.

"I hate doing the windows there," Maggie says. "Do you think that maybe we'll get a break and . . ."

I stop listening, tell myself I'm ready for the Donaldson house. I'll go in, do what I need to, and get out. Just like that. Just that simple.

I tell myself that, but I feel sick when we get there, on edge. It doesn't help that when we pull in I see Allison and James out on the lawn with their parents and a few other people. James is surrounded by most of them, and clinging to his arm is a girl staring at him like he's everything. Allison is off on one side smiling like she did when we were talking to the guy with the polo shirt collar problem, a bored, polite smile. She sees me and smiles, really smiles.

I duck my head and pretend I don't see her.

Inside, Joan and I have to clean the downstairs, and she tells me I'm doing the bathroom, study, solarium, dining room, and kitchen and gets pissed when I argue with her. I actually want the rooms—or at least the kitchen—but I don't want Joan to know that. She tells me to quit complaining and get to work already, and I sigh dramatically and say, "Okay, fine, I'm going."

I look outside when I'm done vacuuming. The Donaldsons are all still out on the lawn. Closer to the house, Shelly is leaning against the car we came in, rubbing the small of her back with one hand. Joan and Maggie are there too—Maggie's putting together the long brush we use to clean windows, and Joan is standing a few feet away smoking furiously. I put on my gloves, pull the second bag out of my cleaning duffel, and then head to the kitchen.

The silver is still in the pantry and I start putting it in the bag, moving as quickly and quietly as I can. This is the first job I've done by myself and what I take will decide if Mom and I get to live however and wherever we want for a while, or if we'll be stopping as soon as we can. What I take—

I hear footsteps, then voices.

"I told you I don't have time to talk about this now," James says. He sounds very annoyed and very close. I stare at the silver I'm holding and then crouch down, push myself as far back into the shadows as I can.

"Why did you do it? You knew—you knew the only reason I hadn't told Mom and Dad I was bringing Brad to the party was because I don't care what they think, but you go and tell him it's because I'm embarrassed? How could you? Do I run around asking you what happened with Janet or what's going to happen to whoever you're with today? Do I . . ."

Allison's voice cracks. "Do I ever say anything? All the stuff you do, that you've done and I've never—"

"You're not thinking," James says softly. "If you were you'd see . . . look, don't—Ally, don't cry. You are who you are and you just—you can't ignore it even if you want to."

"I'm not you. Don't you get that? I'm not like you; I don't want to be like you."

I hear her footsteps race across the floor, then a door slam. I hear James sigh and then, after a few seconds, he walks off too. I wait a little bit and then stand up, move out of the pantry, and look cautiously out a window. James is back on the lawn, laughing and gesturing at everyone gathered around him, the girl from before standing there like she's just waiting for him to see her. Allison is on the edge of the group, trying to smile. She looks miserable. I know how she feels. I know—my stomach knots up.

I know how she feels because I hate this.

I know how she feels because I hate this life.

The bag slides out of my hands and onto the floor. I stand there looking at it, at what's inside it. The silver lying there isn't mine.

I don't want to do this.

I have to do this. Mom is waiting for me, counting on me. I zip the bag up. My hands, encased in gloves, look like they could belong to someone else. I wish they did. I know they don't.

I drop the bag by my other one, take a deep breath, and then pick up the one with all my cleaning stuff in it. I find Shelly and tell her I'm quitting. She shrugs, says, "Right now?" and when I say "Yeah," and drop my bag on the floor, she gives me a "So what?" look and then goes back to cleaning. I walk through the house, picking up the other bag on the way. I don't see anyone. I'm careful not to. I walk out the front door. The bag is heavy on my shoulder.

Outside I head down the driveway. I avoid looking at the lawn, at anything but the road that's waiting for me.

"Hey, are you leaving?"

I stop, don't let myself close my eyes. "Hey, Allison." I should look at her but I can't.

"You're not leaving with everyone else?"

"I quit."

"Just now?"

I nod.

"Oh. I'm sorry. You've still got your gloves on. Did you burn your hands or something?"

"I'm fine. Just forgot to take them off."

"Oh," she says again. "Okay. I—well, the thing is I kind of need to talk to Brad and I don't know what to say. I mean, I know what I want to say but—well, you know how it is — and I was thinking maybe we could go somewhere and you can tell me if what I want to say sounds okay or if it sounds—"

"Stop." I shift my weight and the bag swings a little, the silver making a soft clinking sound. "I can't, okay? I wish—I wish I could. But I can't."

I walk away. I tell myself I don't feel bad for what just happened, for what I'm doing, for what I'm carrying slung over my shoulder. I tell myself this is how things are. How they should have been all along. How they always will be. It's that simple and there's nothing I can do to change it.

Even if I wish there was.

24

Mom is waiting for me just down the road.

"Baby," she says when she sees me, and then slides on a pair of latex gloves. She takes the bag, puts it in the trunk. I hand her my gloves when she shuts it, watch her peel off her own and then disappear up over the hill she's parked next to. I can hear, faintly, the roar of the ocean.

She comes back empty-handed. I'm already in the car, and when she gets in she leans over and kisses my cheek. "You did a good job, baby."

I nod, look out the window. I watch everything blur as we drive, picking up speed.

"Hey, you okay?"

"I—" I'll never know what I might have said because blue lights flash then, around and around and right behind us.

Cops.

Mom slows down, pulling the car over to the side of the road. "No matter what, you keep your mouth shut. Got it?"

I nod, scared by her voice, by what's going on. This has never happened before.

Mom turns the car off. The blue lights are still on, still flashing. I hear the crunch of footsteps as the cop moves closer, and then it hits me, really hits me. We've been pulled over. We have stolen silver in the trunk. We've been *caught*.

Suddenly everything seems too loud, too bright. My hands are shaking. I try to press them against my knees and can't. They're shaking too hard. I look at Mom. She's rolled her window down and is sitting relaxed, one arm resting on it, fingers dangling out for the wind to catch them. She's looking at a cop who is looking back at her. At me.

"Ma'am?" the cop says.

He starts talking and I see Mom nodding, smiling. Maybe everything will be okay. She'll get the cop to smile, to laugh. He'll tell us to have a nice day as he walks away. He'll do that and we'll start the car again, drive down the road and away, away.

"I'm going to need you to get out of the car now, ma'am. And you too, miss," the cop says loudly. It changes everything. I can tell because I see Mom's hand, still resting lightly against the window, twitch once. Her hands have always been steady before.

We get out of the car. The cop asks Mom for identification. She smiles, all charm. "I seem to have left my license at home. I'm so sorry. Is that what this is about? I think it's a good thing that you're cracking down on this, I do, and I swear, normally I always carry my license with me but today I was in such a rush—"

"Miss?" the cop says, turning away from Mom like she hasn't spoken at all. I watch her smile fade. "Do you have any identification on you?"

I shake my head. I have nothing on me and haven't since I tossed my phone this morning. Mom will have mailed the few things we'll need wherever we end up to our fence, who'll hold it for us. Everything else—all the clothes, all the food, her phone, everything—has all been disposed of. We have nothing now except for what's in the trunk.

The cop clears his throat. "I'm going to have to search your car."

223

No. No no no no no no. I was careful, so careful, kept my gloves on the whole time, but the silver is in the trunk and there's not going to be a way to explain it, not going to be a way—

"No," my mother says, and her voice is soft but steel strong. "I don't give you permission to search my car. In fact, I'd like to know why you pulled us over in the first place. I mean, since when is just driving suspicious?"

The cop ignores her and looks through the car. He's methodical about it and keeps pausing to look at us, watching our faces.

His radio crackles. He goes back to his car for a second and says something into it, then comes back and reaches into our car, popping open the trunk. When he does that, Mom smiles.

I don't get it. How can she smile?

The cop pulls out the bag. He says, "What's this." It's not a question. He knows he's found something. Mom is still smiling.

"Mom?" I whisper, and then she turns that smile toward me. It doesn't reach her eyes, which are warning me to keep quiet. I close my mouth and watch as she turns away, still smiling. I watch the cop unzip the bag, see his eyes widen as he looks inside.

"Well," he says. "Don't suppose you have a receipt for all this?" When neither of us say anything he nods, smiling like he's won the lottery. "Looks like I'm going to have to take you both in."

Mom laughs. It's the happiest I've heard her sound in ages and I realize she's enjoying this. I watch her and know that no matter what she says, no matter what I do, I will never truly be like her. I'll never want anything like this. I'll never enjoy it. This—it could never make me happy. Not ever.

"My daughter and I both want a lawyer," she says, putting an arm around me. "We have one, and I'm going to need to contact him right away."

The cop's smile fades. "Sure, though I have to warn you, I don't think anyone will be able to explain this away. Maybe you'd like to say something now, help me—"

"I'm sorry," Mom says. "I guess I wasn't clear enough. I wish to contact our attorney immediately."

The cop shrugs and then he is saying things like "Do you understand?" This can't be real, I think, but then he says, "felony burglary" loudly and I know it is.

"Are you ladies ready?" the cop asks when we're

cuffed and in his car. My mother laughs again, shaking her head so that her hair falls perfectly around her face. I stare at the floor, and as we start to move I feel sick. I scoot as close to her as I can, wanting to be near her, wanting her to tell me everything will be all right.

She doesn't look at me. She's talking easily, so beautiful and so charming. I hear the cop tell her his name is Joe and that he's got three kids, all boys.

"Always wanted a daughter," he says. "How long have you two lived here?"

My mother smiles and asks about his boys. She looks so calm and I can tell, by the way she is sitting, legs lightly crossed and head turned so the sun catches and shows the dark brilliance of her hair, that she is. She is sure everything will be fine.

I am hunched forward, conscious of every car we pass, of every rattle the bag makes as it shifts in the front seat. I watch the cop's eyes flicker toward it once, twice. I watch him smile.

I'm not sure of anything.

25

I start to shake when we reach town, when the police station gets closer and closer, becoming all I can see. The cop parks and gets out of the car. He picks up the bag, and I hear the silver shift inside.

"Keep quiet and everything will be fine," Mom whispers, comfort and warning in her voice. I press my hands back into the circle of metal that holds them, do it over and over until the skin around my wrists starts to hurt.

Mom's taken out of the car first. I start shaking more. Even my teeth are doing it now, chattering like I'm caught in a snowstorm. It sounds weird. No one seems to hear it but I press my teeth together anyway, so hard I hear them click.

Mom doesn't look back as she's led away. I'm helped out of the car next. My legs don't give out on me even though I'm sure they will. I stare at the back of Mom's head, not wanting to see who is steering me inside, when it occurs to me, suddenly, that it could be Greg. My stomach lurches and I quickly look over.

It isn't him.

I'm sure I'll see him though. I'm sure he'll look at me and see who I am, who I really am, and the strange thing between us will turn into something I know. It will become nothing but a look like the ones I'm getting from everyone we pass.

Inside the station I see stairs, which I'm not taken up, and a hallway, which I'm led down. I don't see Mom anymore.

"You asked for a lawyer?" a man says as soon as I'm led into a room, his voice loud and fast and disbelieving. When I don't respond he moves in closer, so close all I see are his bloodshot eyes. "You asked for a lawyer? First thing? You sure about that?"

I take a step back and shake my head. The man talking to me is pissed off, red-faced to match his eyes. His voice is even louder when he speaks again.

"So is that a yes? A no?"

"Yes. I'm sure."

More staring, some muttering, and then the start of what I can tell is a frequently given "warning" about "wet-behind-the-ears" public defenders. The cop who brought Mom in comes by and says something. Not to me, of course, but the man stops his speech midsentence and I'm led into another room.

Mom once told me that being arrested was a lot like waiting in line. I thought that was a strange thing to say but she's right. Getting arrested is—past the initial part, the part where I stood and watched that cop lift up the bag and felt everything inside me shatter—boring.

First, I'm searched by a female cop who says nothing except, "The duffel that came in with you—that's yours, right? You want me to add it to the list of your possessions?"

How stupid does she think I am?

The kind of stupid that tosses a bag loaded with silver into the back of a car, I guess. But still, that's the kind of question I knew not to answer from the time I was old enough to talk. I pretend to be fascinated by my shoes. Eventually she realizes I'm not going to answer and I'm led back out into the hallway.

Next is forms and fingerprinting and then more

forms and photos. There's a lot of waiting around during each of these things, a lot of time where nothing much seems to happen and whoever I'm with looks at me like I'm supposed to say something. The questions I know I can answer I do, and the others I ignore.

Finally, after being asked, "Is there anything you want to say? You sure? Nothing you want to talk about?" about a million times, I'm taken into a room. It's awful: no windows, industrial green walls, and the only furniture is a battered table and chairs. It also smells terrible, like sweat, and it's hot. I'm told to sit down and then I'm left alone.

There's no clock, so I have no idea what time it is or how long I sit for. Sweat gathers under the armpits of my polyester nightmare yellow dress, behind the backs of my knees. Eventually it gathers behind my shoulder blades and drips down my back. I shift in the chair. It makes a sad groaning noise. Eventually another cop comes in and offers me a sandwich and something to drink "if I want."

I shake my head no and am left alone again.

The sandwich-offering cop comes back after I've counted the number of scratches on the table four times. (Two hundred and twelve. Two hundred and thirteen if you count the one that branches off as two.) He's carrying a coffee mug. I can smell the coffee in it, see it slosh against the rim when he sits down across from me.

"So . . ." A pause, and I press my hands together, waiting. "I guess you know this isn't the first time your mother has been arrested."

I nod.

"And your father? Heard from him recently?"

I'm silent, force myself to sit perfectly still, to not show any reaction at all.

"Right," the cop says, after taking a sip from his mug. "Sorry about that. Guess it's just you two then. You like it around here?"

I shrug, and the cop leans toward me. I can smell the coffee on his breath. "Here's the thing. You're eighteen now and—"

"And since I am I can be charged as an adult, but guess what? If I know something, you could help me out."

"You're young. You got caught up in something you had no control over. You don't owe your mother anything—"

I laugh, watch the cop's coffee mug pause midway to his mouth. "I owe her everything."

"You misunderstand me," the cop says, and puts the mug down, leaning in toward me again. "No one's blaming you here. No one's saying you were a part of anything. Your mother—well, she's a very persuasive woman and . . ."

I stare at him, silent. A frown creases his forehead and he leans back in his chair. We look at each other for a moment and then he smiles at me.

"I guess you also know your mother recently had all her assets placed under your name, right? And since she's done that, now that you're an adult, should anything illegal or improper ever show up—"

I try really hard not to look surprised but know I fail. I knew Mom had some stuff set aside in case of an emergency, but why would she put it in my name?

"Think about it," the cop says. "She decides to put everything in your name and now you're here? Maybe—"

"Maybe what?"

The cop shrugs.

"She loves me. She would never hurt me."

"What do you call this?" The cop gestures around

the room, at himself and then at me. "You think this is what people who love their kids want for them? You think getting caught with—" There's a knock on the door and the cop breaks off.

"Look, if you want to talk about what happened earlier—" Another knock on the door and he throws up his hands and leaves, biting off, "Think about what I said," before he goes.

After he's gone I count the scratches on the table again. I know for a fact Mom doesn't believe in love. But she's kept me with her, kept me even when Dad decided I was old enough to be on my own, that I was a burden he didn't want—not even for a little while—anymore.

What the cop just told me—Mom has a reason for it, I know it. She may not believe in love, but she's shown it. My whole life, she's the only one who has. And that wouldn't end now. It won't.

At some point—my guess is after the night shift starts—I finally say yes to the offer of a sandwich. It arrives in a crumpled bag resting in Greg's hands. I was starving but as soon as I see him—and the look on his face—my stomach shrivels up. I look down at the table, watch the bag come to rest in front of me.

"Did anyone get you a soda?" I can't tell anything from his voice. I am used to hearing it full of laughter or exasperation or something I could never quite name, but now it's flattened out, gone official. I think about the day we went to Edge Island, of what I said to him, of what he said to me. He knew something was going on with me. I thought—I don't know what I thought. I wouldn't let myself think about it, would I? But he knew I was hiding something, and now I have to wonder if he's been waiting for this moment.

I look at him.

He looks tired, his face and hair washed out by the shitty lighting. He looks . . . sad.

"I don't need one," I tell him. "I'm fine."

He doesn't say anything for a moment, just looks at me. "You sure?" he says, and the expression on his face is the one I could never quite name, except now I finally know what it is. I recognize it from how I look after I talk to Mom sometimes, a lot of times.

Worry.

Care.

I manage to nod and then I have to look back down at the table. Eventually he leaves. I open the bag and pull out the sandwich. I try to eat it. It's hard for me to swallow. There's a knot in my throat, in my stomach. I put the sandwich down on top of the bag.

After a while another cop comes in and asks if I need to use the bathroom. I tell her I do and she asks if I'm finished, pointing at the sandwich. I nod, watch as she sweeps it into the bag. As we walk to the bathroom she tosses it into a trash can. She smells like coffee too. No wonder I've never been able to drink the stuff.

The bathroom is the same horrible green as the room I've been in. I go and then sit there staring at my feet, at the hem of my yellow uniform bunched up around my thighs. I can hear the cop outside talking to someone. She laughs and then the door opens. She says, "Hurry up in there."

I say, "Okay" and stand up. The door opens and swings shut again. I guess I'm not hurrying fast enough. I sigh and flush, walk out of the stall. As I'm washing my hands I see a soda resting on the floor right by the door. Regular, not diet. I know who put it there and suddenly I am biting the inside of my cheek hard, and blinking as fast as I can, my eyes burning.

I go over and pick up the can. I open it. I close

my eyes and lean against the wall. The soda is cold and sweet and when I'm done I throw the can away and spit in the sink. A trail of brownish pink snakes across it. I turn on the water and wash it away.

The cop gives me a long stare when I come out but doesn't say anything. She doesn't take me back to the room, just motions for me to sit down by a desk before she turns away to talk to someone. I watch people walk by and look at me. For about half a second I wonder what they're thinking, but it's totally obvious, and so I turn away from all the faces and look at the desk. There's not much to see. Lots of papers, mostly.

My name is on one of the papers. I pretend to yawn, glance at the cop. She's still talking, though her gaze does flicker to me for a second. She probably wants me to read whatever this is—I know how cops are—and so I shouldn't, but I can't help myself.

It's notes of some sort, and there's mention of time of arrival, of people present. Joan Walter, Maggie Ramone, Allison Donaldson, Shelly Stubbson . . . this is definitely about me. About—I look over at the cop again. She's sitting down now, talking on the phone and snapping her fingers at someone walking by. I turn back to the paper.

Joan, Maggie, and Shelly didn't see anything. Maggie volunteers that I always said I didn't like my uniform. Shelly says I told her I quit and that I "dumped her cleaning bag on me! Like I need to be carrying extra weight around. Can I sit down now? My back is killing me." Joan says, "Well, she can't clean a toilet to save her life, but she's an okay kid. You got any cigarettes?"

Allison says she and I talked and that she saw me leave. She didn't see me carry anything out. I read that last sentence again.

Miss Donaldson didn't see the suspect carrying anything when she left.

I read more.

I said, "You sure she wasn't carrying anything? A bag, maybe?"

"No. She didn't have anything with her."

I can't believe she said that. I know she saw the bag. I know she must know that I—and she didn't say anything.

I look up and the cop is off the phone, is sitting there watching me. "You doing okay? You look a little upset."

"I'm fine."

"You sure?" She gets up and comes over, squats down next to me. "Look, you seem like a nice kid. I think you've got your mom to deal with and maybe she was anxious about something or pressuring you, and if you want to talk—"

"The last person I'd ever want to talk to is you." I am shaking again but it's not with fear. It's with anger. Anger at this—where I am, what's going on. I'm angry at being asked if I want to talk by people who only want to hear things I'll never say. I'm angry because I talked to Allison with a bag full of silver that belongs to her family in my arms and wasn't even nice to her, didn't try to be the friend I wish I could be. I'm angry because I didn't want to take anything today but I did. I pretended I didn't have a choice but I did. I did.

"Have it your way," the cop says, a scowl darkening her face, and then I'm hauled back to the little green room and left there.

26

The cop from before, the one who led me to the bathroom, comes back after I don't know how long has passed and opens the door, flicks two fingers at me in a "come on, hurry up" gesture. I get up and walk out of the room, wait for her to tell me where I'm going now.

"They're waiting for you down there," she says with a frown, and points to the left before walking off. I can see the sun, just barely rising, out of a far window, which means I've been here all night.

I take a deep breath and head off in the direction the cop told me to go. I pass one room with no cops, then another, and now I'm in a hallway lined with offices. I don't look in any of them, just keep walking. So far, so good. I'm not kidding myself—I'm sure I'm not going anywhere, figure this is something to rattle me—but at least for a second I can pretend I'm leaving.

"Dani?"

I turn around. Greg walks out of an office I just passed, heading toward me.

I open my mouth and then close it because I have no idea what to say. I want to thank him for the soda. I want to ask him why he looked at me the way he did when he gave me the sandwich. I want to go back to when we were just two people standing in a grocery store, all the way back to the beginning. I don't know why I want that. I don't know what I would have done differently. I still want it anyway.

"Are you okay?" he asks.

I have to say something. Anything. "I'm fine."

"You sure?"

Yes. That's all I have to say. But I'm just standing there, silent, because I'm not sure. In fact, if there's one thing I am sure of, it's that everything isn't fine. That I'm not fine.

"Hey," he says, and moves closer. "Dani, look, if you want to talk . . ."

If I want to talk. How many times have I heard

that today? How many times have I heard that my whole life, always from people who wanted to take Mom away from me? Something hot and painful pinches behind my eyes, in my throat, but it's easy for me to speak now.

"If I wanted to talk I'm sure you'd be willing to listen. In fact, I bet that you and everyone here would love to listen. But you know what? I don't want to talk. Especially not to you." I walk off down the hall, not even looking where I'm going.

I can't believe Greg turned out to be just like everyone else and I'm so stupid for being surprised by it, for being hurt by it.

Someone touches my arm, stopping me. Another cop. "You can't be wandering around back here," he says, and points at a door behind me. "Go in there, take a right down the first hall you see, and then another right."

I can't quite bring myself to say thank you—especially because I still don't know where I'm going, but I nod at him and start walking.

"Hey," he calls out.

I knew it. I stop, wait.

"Look," he says, and pulls out a business card. "If you remember something or maybe want to talk . . ." He pushes the card toward me.

Unbelievable. I wonder what he would say if I told him how many cops have said this to me already. He snaps his fingers in front of my face, impatient.

"Hey," he says, voice rising a little. "Look, I'm offering you a chance to do the right thing, so the least you can do is—"

"This," I say, and walk away.

Mom and a lawyer are waiting for me at the end of the hall. I recognize the lawyer right away. It's Dennis, who I remember from a trip Mom and I made to New York when I was twelve. He starts talking—Dennis is very good at talking, I remember that too—and after a moment I realize he's saying that Mom and I can leave. In fact, we are leaving, the three of us heading outside and walking toward Dennis's car.

We aren't being charged with anything. I start to ask why but Mom shoots me a look and I fall silent, stare down at the ground so I won't have to see everyone walking by staring at us.

Dennis takes us to breakfast. Or at least he says he

is, but I bet the whole meal will end up being billed to us. Mom doesn't seem very worried about it. In fact, she and Dennis are both in very good moods, Mom saying, "I always knew you were brilliant, Dennis, but tell us what happened again, will you? I want Danielle to hear this. Baby, listen."

It turns out the cops didn't have a warrant when they searched the trunk. And while cops can search a car if they think there's cause, they can't search a trunk without a warrant or permission. The cop who arrested us didn't know about the silver at all. He pulled us over because someone has been selling coke in Heaven and he'd seen Mom earlier, driving around waiting for me, and decided she was carrying drugs. When he stopped us, he figured we'd rat on each other as soon as he found anything, and so he went ahead and looked in the trunk.

Mom smiles. "He was such a nice man. So very . . . determined. I suppose he won't get that promotion he said he was hoping for."

"I doubt it," Dennis says, and they both laugh. I take a bite of eggs I don't remember ordering and chew and chew and chew. I can't seem to swallow though, finally have to take a big sip of water and let the food wash down my throat. They're still laughing. I don't see what's so funny.

"Baby," Mom says. "You were worried, weren't you?"

"I—a little. I mean, people saw me leaving the house and then the silver was there in the trunk—"

"But you didn't take it," Dennis says. "The bag that held it didn't have your or your mother's fingerprints on it. Neither did the silver. There's simply no way you're responsible for what someone else did when you were at work and your mother left the car unattended to walk on the beach. I know if either of you had seen whoever it was that put the silver in your trunk or if you had opened it and found it, you would have notified the police right away. But you didn't see anything, you left the only black duffel bag you were known to possess with one of your fellow employees when you quit your job, and you certainly didn't know what had happened. So you can't be blamed for anything. Understand?"

I nod because I do understand—I understand that Dennis is a very good lawyer and that I need to keep my mouth shut—and go back to picking at my food. It's hot in here, too hot to eat. I take another sip of water, think of Greg leaving the soda in the bath-room for me, and want to weep. I don't know why he did it. He knows what I did, what I am—and he still did it. Why? I excuse myself and go to the bath-room. It's tiny and even hotter than the restaurant, pink seashell soaps melting in the real shell that holds them. I wash my hands carefully, slowly, and then go back to the table.

Dennis is signaling the waitress for more coffee. I realize everyone is watching us. The noise my chair makes as I pull it out sounds incredibly loud. Mom looks up from her breakfast—mostly untouched, I realize—and smiles at me.

I smile back, say, "You should eat, you know, be-cause if I'm driving we're not stopping at any fast food places for at least a hundred miles."

"What?" She's looking at me like I'm crazy.

"I'm kidding, Mom. We can stop whenever. I'm just . . . I'm really ready to go, you know?" I want to be away from here so bad I can taste it.

"Baby, we aren't leaving now. We're—" Mom stops talking, her face turning bright red. I stare at her, wondering what's going on. Has she seen something or someone? Is she choking? Even Dennis seems to realize something is wrong, looks up from the pan-cakes he's eating and says, "Are you all right?"

Mom nods, shuddering, and after a moment, starts coughing, the sound loud and wet.

"I think you might want to go to a doctor." Dennis seems concerned. He must really cost a lot of money. I keep looking at Mom, waiting for her to smile or say something that will make Dennis and maybe even me laugh, but she doesn't. She doesn't say anything. She just keeps taking deep shuddering breaths.

"I will," she finally says, the words coming out quiet, small, and that's when I know something is wrong. Very wrong.

27

Mom doesn't go to the doctor. After she tells Dennis she will, the two of them start looking at each other in a way that makes me wonder if I'm going to have to spend some time sitting around outside when we get back to the house.

It turns out that I don't, but that's only because Mom comes up to me after inviting Dennis in "to discuss some things" and taps my shoulder, hands me some money, and says, "Go out for a few hours." Before I can even say anything, like ask how I'm supposed to go somewhere without a car—ours certainly isn't anywhere around—or even a phone to call a cab, she's nudging me outside and shutting the door.

So I go out. When I get back Dennis is gone and Mom's sitting outside looking out at the water.

"Did you go to the doctor?" I ask.

She gives me a look.

Of course she didn't. Stupid of me to even ask, but then I'm feeling a little scattered right now.

"Sorry," I mutter and sit down next to her. "I guess you'll go before we leave?"

"Please. I'm fine. Look at me. Do I look sick to you?"

"No, but—"

"I'm fine." She puts an arm around me, pulls me close. "Really, I am. I promise. Okay, baby?"

"Okay." She does seem fine. Maybe I was worried for nothing. I mean, she did look a little strange at breakfast, but then I'd been up for who knows how long, and oh yeah, spent most of that time sitting in a police station. "So, when are we leaving?"

She doesn't say anything.

"Mom?"

"Soon, baby," she says. "I need to take some time, think things over. And right now I need a nap." She leans over and kisses the top of my head, then goes inside.

She never asks where I've been.

This is what happened when I went out:

I walked to the beach. I walked and it felt nice; the wind was blowing, not hard but just enough to make it feel like summer, and the sun was shining strong and bright.

I could hear the ocean the whole way there too. It got louder as I got closer to the beach. I hadn't ever been to the public one. I'd driven by it, talked to—talked to Allison about it—but I'd never gone. It was crowded and as I walked down the street that ran alongside it I felt like just another tourist, walking around staring at the signs for food and fun and T-shirts. The whole place even smelled like the beach, like suntan lotion and sand and the sea.

I stopped at one place, a hamburger stand, thinking I'd get something to eat since I hadn't eaten much breakfast. I ended up buying just a soda because the girl who was working the cash register stared at me like I was a ghost.

"You're that thief," she said right after she asked what I wanted. She pushed my soda across the counter hard, spilling most of it, and when she gave me my change she wouldn't touch my hand, just dropped coins into it.

I wanted to go home after that but I couldn't.

Well, I could have, but I'd have had to wait around for Dennis to leave and besides, Mom clearly wanted me gone. So I kept walking, but now I noticed everyone who looked at me and then pointed or turned to say something to whoever they were with. I threw my soda away and crossed the street, heading for the beach.

There was a line to get in. A line of cars and even a line of people. The people waiting in front of me —a guy and a girl, clearly together—didn't seem to know who I was. They told me they'd come for "a day of fun" and asked where they could rent an umbrella. They also asked if I knew why the police were there.

"I mean, is there some sort of crime spree going on around here?" the girl said, laughing.

I smiled back, weakly, and thought about getting out of line. But I was too close to the front and I knew walking away would just attract more attention.

There were two cops talking to people. One of them I didn't recognize. The other one was Greg. He was wearing a hat but his nose was sunburned even worse than it had been the day he took me to lunch. I knew I shouldn't have thought about that, should have just thought about what he was, a cop, and nothing more, but then he looked up and saw me.

He smiled. He smiled when he saw me. Not a cop smile, an "I've got my eye on you" smile, but a smile like the ones he'd always given me. A smile that was just a smile. A smile like he was happy to see me.

I stepped out of line then, walked back down the street. When I saw him smile I wanted to smile back. I wanted to ask him about his nose and how his day was and talk like we always did. I was stupid, so stupid. Things could never be like that. Maybe they never were like that.

I knew that was a lie. Somehow, in some strange way, we'd connected. It shouldn't have happened, but it did.

I kept walking. The food stands and souvenir stores disappeared, replaced with houses, the small ones I never paid much attention to before. I looked at them then, really looked at them. Everyone I saw—people hanging up beach towels or looking out at the ocean or even just sitting around—they all seemed happy to be where they were. I wondered what it would be like to feel that way, to be where you were and not worry about what might happen, not always know you'd be moving on. I wished there was a way I could feel like that, even if it was for just a little while.

I walked over to the beach again. It was marked FOR RESIDENTS ONLY but the sign was peeling and hung crookedly, like it had been forgotten. I took off my shoes, felt the sand sink hot under my feet and between my toes. I watched two little kids fight over who was going to fly a kite, then walked down to the ocean. It still wasn't much to look at but then its blankness seemed comforting.

The water was cold, a shock after the warmth of the sand. Nearby I heard a girl laugh, saw her race into the waves, looking over her shoulder to smile at the guy she was with. It was Allison. She stopped smiling when she saw me and walked back onto the beach.

I wasn't surprised to see her. It seemed like it was something that had to happen. She didn't move away as I walked hesitantly toward her, but she didn't look at me either, just stood staring out at the water.

"What are you doing here?" she asked.

"I was out walking and—"

"No. I mean here in town still. After everything you and your mom did, why stay?"

"We're leaving soon." I took a deep breath,

watched as one row of waves hit the shore and then another. "Why did you do it?"

She was quiet for a moment. She didn't ask what I meant.

"I did it because I feel sorry for you," she finally said. "Everything you have isn't real, isn't yours. It'll never be yours. That must really suck."

A guy called her name then, a question in his voice, and I watched her turn and smile at him. I could tell from her smile that he was Brad, knew she'd found the right words to say. I watched him smile back at her.

"You're right," I said, and was surprised to hear my voice crack. "It sucks. And look, I—Allison, we were friends. Maybe we could—"

"I thought we were friends," she said, and finally looked at me. She wasn't smiling anymore. "But we weren't. We never will be."

She walked away. She didn't look back. I watched her go and then I turned around, headed back across the sand. My eyes stung, and I lied to myself, said it was just from the sun.

28

I wake up with a start in the morning, open my eyes to see Mom looking down at me with an expression on her face I can't read. I scramble up off the sofa, head into the kitchen. She doesn't ask why I slept downstairs, just comes in behind me and sits down, looking out the window. The only sound is the coffee brewing and her breathing.

She keeps looking out the window while she drinks her coffee. I refill her mug twice. "I need a few days' rest," she finally says. "I need a chance to tie up some loose ends."

"But we—everyone knows what happened. You won't be able to do anything."

"Is that so?"

"I didn't mean it like that. I—we're not leaving?"

"We are leaving. Just not today."

She's going to try something. Getting away but not getting anything—she'll see that as a challenge. I think of the look on her face when we first drove through Heaven, her expression when she saw all those houses, and know we aren't leaving because she needs to be inside one of those houses and take something before she'll be able to move on.

A couple of days later, everything's still the same. We're still here and Mom still isn't ready to leave. She's been gone a lot and when she's home she's . . . she's not here. I mean, she is, and we still watch movies and I tell her she looks great when she twirls around before she leaves, but that's it.

She won't talk about what happened, not with the silver, not with anything. She just says, "It's over. Sometimes that's how it has to be."

I haven't done anything. I've stayed here. I haven't gone out since that one awful afternoon when I saw Greg and Allison, as if I needed a reminder that everything I've done here has totally turned to shit, as if I hadn't already known that I screwed up and hurt Mom, hurt myself, hurt . . . hurt others. Allison and I could have been friends, real friends. Maybe. I don't know. But that's just the thing. I don't know and I never will. I can't even start to think about Greg. It hurts too much.

This morning Mom slept late and then took a long shower, longer than usual, so long that I heard the hot water pipes squeak in protest. I have coffee waiting for her when she comes downstairs. It takes her forever to walk to the kitchen, her breath coming in slow, straining gasps.

I get up and walk over to her. We have to talk sometime and it might as well be now, but before I can say anything she smiles at me, stops me from talking by pushing my hair back with one hand and saying, "We're going to be all right. You'll see. I'll take care of everything."

I don't believe her. That frightens me. But what frightens me more is that she doesn't sound like she believes it either.

She makes her way to the kitchen and drinks her coffee, then picks up her keys and says she's going out. We have another car now. I don't know what happened to the other one but I suspect Dennis made it disappear, just like he took care of everything else. We had a package from him the other day, a bunch of papers delivered by an overnight service. Mom read them and then had me sign some. I didn't ask why. I kept Dennis's card, though. It was clipped to the stack of papers. His last name is Patterson. His office is still in New York.

I did ask Mom if we'd have to pay for having the papers sent. She rolled her eyes and said, "Baby, he's a lawyer. What do you think?"

After she leaves, I sit down and watch television. It's either talk shows or judge shows and I turn it off, get up, and open a window. I can smell the ocean today. I lie down and listen to it, one arm dangling off the sofa, my fingers tracing patterns across the floor. I still love this house. That's the funny thing about all of this. I know we should be gone and I even wish we were. But when it's quiet like this, when it's just me and I'm tired of thinking about stuff—the thing is, when it's like this, I'm still glad we're here.

I hear a car coming up the driveway. Mom, back already?

It isn't Mom, because it's not her car. It's Greg's.

I start to head upstairs, to pretend I'm not home, but you know what? Forget it. I'm pretty sure I know what this is about, and when he gets out of the car and I see he's in uniform I know I'm right.

And that's fine. I can handle this. I have to. I owe it to Mom.

I walk outside, meet him as he's walking toward the steps.

"Hey," he says, like it's just an ordinary day. "I came by to see if you're okay."

"You mean you came by to make sure we leave town."

"No, I mean I came by to make sure you're okay."

"Dressed like that?"

He looks at me. "I know this is going to sound crazy, but they just don't like it when I wear a clown suit to work."

I start to laugh and then turn it into a cough, stare down at the ground. "What do you want?"

"I thought that maybe —" He clears his throat. "I thought that maybe you might want a hot dog."

"What?"

"I brought some with me. I figured you probably hadn't eaten."

"You brought me food?"

"Yeah."

I look at him and he's staring solemnly at me, his eyes shining brilliant green.

"I haven't eaten," I say, and he smiles, goes to his car, and comes back with a paper bag. He sits down on the steps.

After a moment, I sit down next to him.

"How are you?" He asks me that as I'm finishing my second hot dog. I put my hands on my knees, stare out at the water.

"I—okay, I guess." I wonder how long he's known about me. Did he know before he saw me at the police station? Should I ask?

Do I want to know?

I do.

I take a deep breath. "Did you—when did you know about me? About . . . about what I am?"

"Didn't," he says. "I knew you were hiding something, but figured you and your mom were running from a bad family thing or something. It was a real surprise to see you in the station."

"Oh." He didn't think I was a criminal. He was— when he said he wanted to spend time with me, he really meant it. He always meant everything he said. I dare a look at him. "We're—we're leaving soon. I know someone must want to know that."

"That's not why I'm here."

"Oh," I say again, my heart pounding hard. "But still. We are."

"Where are you going?"

"Nebraska."

"I guess I asked for that. But I'm not asking as a cop. I'm asking for me. I'm asking because I want to know you're going to be okay."

I look at him. He looks steadily back at me.

"I don't know," I tell him. "I never do. We just go somewhere and stay for a while. And then—"

"Can I tell you something?"

"Can I stop you?"

He grins at me, that grin that's gotten to me from the first time I saw him, and then rubs one hand against his knee. "Look, everything that happened, the silver getting stolen and then—" He stops. "I know what you're thinking."

"Yeah?"

"Yeah. You get a little"—he points at my forehead—"crinkle when you're mad. But I'm not here because of that and I think you know it. I came because I . . ." He looks down at the ground, then back at me. "You deserve more than not knowing where you're going or how long you'll be there. Don't you want more? Don't you—?"

"You don't get it. It's all I've ever known. All I've ever had. What you have, what everyone else has, a normal life—I've never had that. I'm never going to fit in anywhere, never going to be able to stop—"

He presses two fingers to my mouth and I stare at him, silenced and waiting, a fierce heat rushing through me.

"You can stop," he says. "You can do whatever you want."

I pull back, startled by what he's said, by how he's made me feel.

"Why? Because you say so?" I'm trying to sound tough but have to settle for surprised and breathless.

He grins. "No. Because you can say so."

29

Mom comes home really late and in a strange mood. She's smiling but it doesn't reach her eyes, just stretches as a false curve across her mouth. She asks me what I'm watching but clearly doesn't listen to my answer, stands next to the sofa with one hand curved tight into it, pressing so hard her fingers sink deep into the cushion.

"Are you okay?"

"I'm fine," she says, but the words come out slowly, strangled and breathless. I turned off all the lights earlier, but in the flickering glow of the talk show that I'm not really watching, her face is strained, lit blue and red and green as she tries too hard to breathe normally. Before I can say anything else she turns away and goes upstairs.

I turn off the television and follow her, but by

the time I get upstairs her bedroom door is closing. I think about saying something, about telling her she has to go to the doctor, and catch the door with one hand. I push it open, peer inside.

Mom hasn't turned on any lights and is standing framed by moonlight coming in through the windows, reduced to nothing but a shadow. I push the door open more, clinging to it like a security blanket, like it will tell me how to say what I want to.

"I'm tired," she says sharply. "I just need some sleep. That's all."

"Mom—"

"I'm tired," she says again, and this time it sounds like a plea. I've never heard her sound like this before. I back out of the room, stand in the hall staring at the door I've pulled closed, at my hand resting on it. Eventually I walk to my room, get ready for bed. I don't sleep.

In the morning I'm up extra early and wait anxiously for Mom to get up. I make coffee, and when it sits so long it gets cold, I dump it out and make more. When she finally comes downstairs she heads for the door and before I can even say a word she calls me over, tells me she's going out, and hands me a cell, saying, "Come get me when I call you, okay?"

I know what this means. She's picked a house, found a collection of silver she wants to hold in her hands but she can't really be serious about this. This area is too small and we're way too well known. I grin at her, or try to, and she just gives me a look.

She's serious.

It hasn't even been two weeks since I walked out of the Donaldsons' with a bag slung over my shoulder and she greeted with me a smile, and now she's going to try and steal silver from someone else? She's been reckless sometimes, but she's never been stupid. But this? This is stupid.

I can't say that to her though. I never would, not before and not now, definitely not now, and so I just stand there looking at the cell she's given me and listening to her breathe. She sounds normal today. Maybe that's a sign. Maybe things will be okay.

She doesn't say good-bye. She just leaves. After she's gone I put on my shoes and then take them off. I put the car key in my pocket and then decide to leave it on the hook by the front door. I pick up Dennis's card and fold it into thirds. I put it in my pocket.

I turn the television on and flip through the channels, then turn it off. I make a peanut butter sandwich and eat half of it, tearing the crusts into smaller and smaller pieces. I walk around the house. I get the car key and put it back in my pocket. I make sure the cell is on.

I take Dennis's card out of my pocket and fold it into thirds the other way, then put it back in my pocket. I check to make sure the cell is on again.

I can't stand this. I want to go out and find her. I want to—I don't want to help her. I should, but I don't. I want to leave town. I want to stop this, stop all of it.

I want to stop. I wonder what she would say if I told her that.

I shouldn't say it.

I want to, though.

Why hasn't she called?

I put my shoes back on. I open the window and try to listen to the ocean. I shut the window and turn the television back on. I watch and walk around and around the room, waiting. The afternoon lasts forever, four o'clock creeping to ten minutes after, crawling to fourteen minutes after. At four thirty I make another sandwich, but can only eat half of it again.

At twenty minutes after five I decide I won't say anything. I'll just pick her up when she calls. Things will be better after we get out of here. Everything will go back to normal. I just want to see her. At five thirty I take the phone and go outside, get in the car. I start it.

I can't leave, can't go looking for her. Mom's never been much for rules, but one of the few she's always made me swear to follow is that no matter what, I will always wait for her. I've done this all my life. I've waited and she's always come back. Always. I go back in the house. Twenty minutes till six.

"Ring," I tell the phone. It doesn't. I think about saying it again but I can guess what will happen.

The phone does ring, finally, at seventeen minutes past six. I answer it before the first ring has even stopped. "Where are you?"

There's silence for a moment, and then an unfamiliar voice says, "I'm calling from the emergency room at Provincetown Hospital."

The voice keeps talking but there's a roaring in my

ears like the ocean but louder, a million times louder, and it's all I can hear. The voice keeps talking and I catch a few words, feel them smash into me.

Collapsed

Difficulty breathing

Emergency procedure

I hear a strange brittle snap and realize I'm holding the phone so tight it's cracking around the seam that holds both halves together.

"Are you there?" the voice says, and now it sounds a little unsure. "Are you a family member? It was hard to understand what she was saying when we asked who we should contact and—"

"Mom," I manage to say. "She's my mom."

The voice tells me how to get to the hospital, talks about exits and the interstate. I want to ask how Mom got there but the words won't come. I just hold the phone in my hand while I walk to the car, nodding as I listen to the directions as if the voice can see me. The voice cuts off, the phone going silent as I'm halfway down the driveway, and I have to stop at the end of it because I don't know where to go, have forgotten where all the roads are, forgotten where each one leads.

I stare at the phone. It tells me "call ended." I'm waiting for my mind to wake up, to remember, and then all the words I heard come back, *collapsed emergency procedure difficulty breathing*, and I drive.

30

Once, when I was younger, Mom sent me to the library to do research and I ended up reading a book instead. I don't remember who wrote it but the cover had a girl on it. She was standing in the middle of a grassy field and it looked like she was staring off into the distance but I could tell she wasn't. She had this look on her face, a look I couldn't place but somehow knew, and so I pulled the book off the rack it was sitting on and read it.

It sucked. The girl lived in the country like a hundred years ago and spent all her time thinking about being a schoolteacher. That was it. That was the whole story. I stopped halfway through and looked at the cover again. I would have pulled it off the book and taken it with me, but there was a woman sitting across from me with a little kid in her arms, staring at me like she knew what I was thinking. I put the book back and walked away, but I never forgot that girl's face.

It wasn't even a real face, just some picture, but I still never forgot it. And when I walk into the hospital I realize why I didn't. In the clear glass of the sliding doors that girl's face looks back at me. The girl on the cover of that book was frightened. She'd seen something happen, something that had scared her, and all she could do was wait for what came next.

The doors slide open and I walk inside.

There's fluid in Mom's lungs. A lot of fluid. So much fluid that the emergency clinic she was first taken to had to send her here. This is all I'm told, first by a nurse and then by a doctor. The doctor asks me a bunch of questions, though. Has Mom been coughing? How long has she been coughing? Has she fainted? Had any dizzy spells? Shortness of breath? Stomach problems? Any irregular bleeding? He nods after everything I say, even when I say, "I don't know." The only time he doesn't nod is when I tell him I want to see her.

That gets me an actual reply. A "No, not at this time."

I can't see Mom because the fluid in her lungs is being removed. The doctor doesn't tell me this. He's already gone. The nurse tells me. It's this same nurse who tells me what happened, steering me toward the waiting room as she explains that my mother collapsed while walking down a street and ended up here.

I stare at the nurse. That's not the whole story. I want to know everything. Where exactly was Mom? Did she stop and sink slowly to the ground? Or did it happen suddenly, her whole body giving way like something inside her was broken? Did she say anything when she was found? What does "difficulty breathing" mean? Why does she have to undergo an emergency procedure? But the nurse is already turning away.

If Mom were here she'd tell me not to call attention to myself. She'd tell me to wait, just like she did this morning.

I follow the nurse. I tell her I want to ask a few questions. She smiles at me tiredly. She says she has other patients. I say, "I'll wait." She says someone will be with me soon. I say, "I just want to know what happened to her."

The nurse frowns. I don't move. I say, "Please." I

say, "She's my mother." I say, "I'm scared."

The nurse tells me everything she knows. My mother was found in Heaven, outside a house, by a boy walking his dog. She was lying on the ground. No one saw her fall. She couldn't catch her breath, couldn't talk to the boy, and then she couldn't breathe. An ambulance was called. The paramedics who picked her up heard the fluid in her lungs. There was so much of it the emergency clinic sent her straight here.

"She'll be all right," the nurse says, and pats my arm. I think I want to hug her.

Then she makes me go to the waiting room, and I change my mind about wanting to hug her because I end up sitting next to a man holding a screaming baby. The man seems too tired or too stunned to do anything about it, just stares blankly in front of him. After an hour of this—me sitting, the man staring, and the baby screaming—the man and the baby are finally called back to see a doctor. I watch a television with no sound after that, stop looking at the clock once another hour has passed. I don't want to think about what all this time means.

Finally I'm called back. The doctor is waiting for

me. He takes me inside one of the little cubicles they use for patients and closes the green curtain partway. It rattles as it slides into place.

"We removed the fluid from your mother's lungs," he says. "It doesn't look good. We're running more tests now. Do you have insurance?"

"What doesn't look good?"

"The fluid."

"It was in her lungs. How could it possibly look good?"

The doctor sighs, rubs the bridge of his nose with two fingers. "Fluid in the lungs can be caused by many things. But your mother's lungs contained the kind of fluid that we normally only see in cancer patients."

"Cancer?"

"We won't know anything till we run more tests. In the meantime, your mother was in no shape to fill out forms when she came in but . . ." The doctor trails off and gives me a look. When I don't say anything, he nods like everything is settled, like everything is fine, and walks off.

"Cancer?" I say again, but he doesn't hear me. I say it again, not a question this time. "Cancer." It can't be. It can't.

It could be. After staring blindly at the forms I'm given when I'm taken back to the waiting room, I realize I have to do something. This isn't a job gone bad, this isn't us having to lay low for a while. This is different. I have to make plans. I have to take care of things. Mom isn't going to come along and fix everything this time.

I go outside and notice it's dark, the stars shining dimly overhead, burned out by the glow of the parking lot lights, and get the cell out of the car before I realize I don't know who to call.

I don't know what to do. I walk around the car on rubbery legs, thinking.

We don't have insurance. I don't have any money, and I doubt what Mom has in the house will cover anything.

We need money.

I shove my hands in my pockets. My hands brush against a piece of paper. A card. Dennis's card.

I remember what the cop said about Mom and me and money. I pull out the card. I call the number on it.

I talk to what seems like four hundred people before someone, finally, takes my number and says they'll call me right back.

Fifteen minutes, no call. I go back inside the waiting room. I wish I could rip all the NO CELL PHONES! signs off the wall. The nurse I speak to says she doesn't know anything about Mom. I wish I could rip her head off.

I go back outside. Thirty minutes. No phone call, and there's still no word on my mother.

Dennis calls after fifty-three minutes. He says he's in the middle of a very important business dinner. I hear music in the background. I hear a woman laughing.

"Well?" Dennis says. He sounds annoyed. I tell him what's happened. There is silence for a moment and then he says, "Oh no," in a cracking voice and, "Hold on" to whomever he's with. The next time he speaks, all I hear is his voice.

"Cancer? It could be cancer? It can't be. Not—"

"I know," I say, and wonder if every man Mom has met has fallen in love with her. Stupid of me to even wonder. Of course they have. "I need money to pay for everything. What do I do?"

He starts talking. I listen. I even take notes, jotting them down on the last map Mom stuck in the glove compartment. I write all over New England and am dipping down into North Carolina by the time Dennis is done. I hang up and my legs still feel rubbery and Mom—I wish they'd tell me something. I wish they'd let me see her.

But I have money now. Or will. Dennis said he'd take care of everything with the hospital and that there'd be a package waiting for me at the house when I—Dennis had paused then and hastily added, "When you both get home."

"Right," I said, and wondered if I sounded as fake as he did.

I go back into the hospital, stay in the waiting room staring at the silent television until a nurse comes out and tells me I should go home.

"Shower, get some sleep, eat something," she says. "We'll know more when you get back, I promise."

I don't believe her but I leave, am surprised the sun is up, that it's day again. I drive back to the house. It still looks the same. I feel cheated by this. It should look different.

There are two things by the front door. One is a piece of paper folded in half and taped to the door. The second is an envelope, one of those thin special delivery ones. I pull the paper off the door and open it. Written on it is a phone number. Below it is a name. Greg. I stare at it for a moment and then fold it back in half.

I pick up the envelope, which is stamped RUSH and has a return address in New York. It seems too soon for it to be here, but the fact the sun is shining in my eyes tells me hours have passed since I talked to Dennis. All this time, and Mom—I lean against the door, close my burning eyes. They still hurt when I open them.

Inside the envelope is a note. Dennis's handwriting is large, his letters all slanted sharp. He's had Lucy take care of everything with the hospital. I wonder if I should wonder who Lucy is. I decide I just don't care.

The only other thing in the envelope is a checkbook. The checks have my name on them. There's other stuff too, but I can't get past seeing that. What the cop said is true. Mom put everything in my name. I flip through the thing where you're supposed to write your checks down. It must be called something, but I don't know what it is. Dennis has written a figure at the very beginning, at the top of the first page. I stare at it.

I close the checkbook. I open it again. The figure doesn't change. It can't be right. I fumble for my phone, for Dennis's card.

Dennis says it's right. He says Mom is a "very shrewd investor." He says he's glad the package arrived. He says this in such a way I know I'm supposed to be impressed with how fast he got it here and say so. I'm silent. Dennis clears his throat and asks if I need anything else.

"No," I say, and end the call. We never had to come here. We never had to—we could have stopped somewhere, stayed. We could have found a place and made it our home, a real home.

Mom would never want that.

No. Not would. Not in the past. Will. She will never want that.

I unlock the door and go inside. I should take a shower, eat something, do something, but I don't. I just stand there for a while, a pile of money in one hand and a cop's phone number in the other. It should be funny, shouldn't it? It doesn't feel funny. I let them both go. The checkbook falls straight to the floor. The paper takes a while longer to get there, but I wait, watch it flutter down.

I take a shower and make coffee. I gag with every sip but manage to drink a cup. I pick up the checkbook. I look at the piece of paper on the floor. I pick it up too. I crumple it. It rests in my hand, ready to be thrown away.

I take it out to the car with me, shove it under the seat. At the traffic light I'm forced to sit through before I can turn in to the hospital parking lot, I pick it up and smooth it out. The light is still red. I fold it in half, carefully, and slide it into my pocket.

The light turns green.

31

I'm finally allowed to see Mom. She's still in the emergency room and when I walk into the little green-curtained cubicle that's hers, it's clear what she's expecting. She's ready to leave, is dressed and flipping through a ratty-looking magazine with one hand, the fingers of the other tapping impatiently against her knee.

"You should go start the car," she tells me when she hugs me, a whisper in my ear right after she says "Baby!" and pulls me into her arms. When I don't reply, she moves away and looks at me.

"I want to talk to the doctor," I tell her.

She sighs. "I don't know what they told you, but it's nothing. I'm fine now. Don't I sound fine?"

"You sound terrible."

"I mean aside from sounding like I had a tube

shoved down my throat. Come here, listen." I do, and she breathes slow and deep, easily. Normally. "See? I'm fine."

"So you didn't pass out and have a bunch of fluid pumped out of your lungs?"

"I fainted, probably because I hadn't eaten anything. And the fluid—baby, you know I had that awful cough. And yes, you were right, I should have listened to you and taken more of that medicine." She smiles at me. I fold my arms across my chest. She sighs again.

"I'd think you'd be happy. I'm finally ready to leave. We'll go somewhere new and all you have to do is—"

"They said something about cancer."

"Of course they did. That's how doctors are, baby. If they said everything was fine, how on earth would they stay in business?"

"He said they were going to run some other tests. What were they?"

She leans in toward me. "If we stay here much longer," she whispers, "they're going to figure out we don't have insurance. And that is not—"

"They already know."

"They know?"

"Don't worry. It's taken care of. I called Dennis."

"What?" Her voice rises, becomes sharp. "Why did you do that? What on earth were you thinking? Danielle, you know better than to—"

"Am I interrupting?" The doctor has arrived, and his question isn't really a question, is just a way for him to announce that he's here and ready to talk to us.

"Of course not," my mother says. She smiles at the doctor, but her eyes stay sharp and disappointed, focused on me.

The doctor starts talking. At first it's okay because he repeats what I already know. The passing out, which my mother sighs through. The fluid in the lungs, and how it looked a little odd. That's what the doctor says. "A little odd."

I wait for Mom to say something, but she's staring at the awful green curtain the doctor has pulled all the way closed, a strange pinched look on her face.

That's when I know she has cancer. Before the doctor even says it's "a possibility," I know. And worse, I know Mom knows too. I sit down, stumble back onto a hard orange plastic chair.

The doctor keeps talking. He shows us pictures

of Mom's lungs. He shows us a dark spot, a shadow. He says, "We need to run more tests, find out exactly what we're dealing with. We're going to admit you." He's talking to Mom but she isn't looking at him, is still staring at the curtain. The doctor doesn't seem surprised, just turns and starts talking to me.

"It's best to be as aggressive as possible when it comes to this sort of thing," he says, and points at the picture of Mom's lungs again, tapping two fingers against the shadow as if I've somehow forgotten it's there. "We won't know anything for sure until we've done more tests, but this, along with the results of the blood work we've run, indicates that time—"

"Thank you," Mom says, and her smile is radiant, beautiful enough to convince anyone of anything. "But is all this necessary for a little spot? I mean, really."

The doctor just looks at her.

Mom's smile fades. "It's not just a spot." She picks up a magazine and starts reading. The doctor looks at her for a moment more and then turns back to me.

"We're going to do the very best we can. We'll send someone down to move your mother up to a room shortly."

* * *

It's cancer. After two days that word becomes my whole world. Two days, Mom sitting silent in a hospital room and looking at me like I've let her down. Two days, and I sleep in uncomfortable chairs, go home when I'm told to, and come back as soon as I can. Two days, and the doctor says a lot of words I don't know and that Mom doesn't ask any questions about. Two days, and at the end of them someone says something to me as I stumble down the hall trying to remember where the vending machines are and wondering what metastasized means.

"Excuse me," I hear, and turn around to see the doctor looking at me.

"Might I have a word with you?" he says, and before I can say anything he starts talking. He tells me Mom seems uninterested in what's happening to her. He says this occasionally occurs and he certainly understands, but that time is very important here.

He says, "Do you understand what I'm saying?"

"No," I say, and then he tells me.

Mom's cancer has spread. The spot on her lung is from the spreading. She needs treatment right away. Aggressive treatment. Chemotherapy. "I want to get started immediately," the doctor says, "but she won't consent to anything. She needs to agree to this. Do you understand?"

"Yes," I say, because now I do.

I go back to Mom's room. She glances at me when I come in, then goes back to reading magazines. Today she's reading a cooking magazine. I sit down on her bed, turn so I am facing her.

"I just talked to the doctor."

She keeps reading her magazine.

"Do you want to know what he said?"

She puts the magazine down. "Do you know what I hate most about this place? I hate how everyone talks to me. The nurses, the doctors. You. How am I feeling? Do I need anything? Do I have any questions? Do I understand what's going on? Let me ask you a question. Do you think this place has anything I could ever be interested in? Do you think I want to sit here day after day after day? Do you?"

I shake my head, suddenly close to tears.

"Oh baby," she says. "Don't look like that. I just want to get out of here. I want you to stop rushing around writing checks every thirty seconds. I want to be in the car with the wind in my hair and the radio on. I don't—" I hear her take a deep breath, hear the slight rattling sound of it. "I don't want this."

"You need to . . ." I don't know how to say this. "The doctor says—"

"I know. I need chemotherapy. But to stay here? To sit here day after day with tests and tubes and this?" She gestured around the room.

"What if we go somewhere else?" Her eyes light up and I continue. "There must be other hospitals, better ones. I'll find out and we'll pick one, go there."

The light in her eyes dims. "Another hospital."

"A better one."

She laughs a laugh that isn't one at all. "Then you'll be writing checks every fifteen seconds."

I look down at the bed. "We have money." I try to keep my voice even but she knows me. Of course she does.

"It's for the future. Not for me to sit here and read crappy magazines and eat even crappier food in a place where a room with a view gets you—" She looks out the window. "A Dumpster." She laughs, for real this time. "That just figures, doesn't it?"

I look at her. "Why won't you do this?"

"Because," she says angrily, and then stops. She reaches out and cups my chin in one hand. Her fingers are cool. I close my eyes.

"Please," I say.

She is silent for a long time. I feel her fingers drop away from my chin and squeeze my eyes closed harder, like I did when I was young and would lie in bed waiting for her to come home.

"All right," she says quietly, and I open my eyes.

32

I call Greg that night. I don't know why but I do, stand outside the front door and unfold the piece of paper with his name scrawled across it. It's only when he answers the phone sounding like he's asleep that I realize how late it is, that it's dark, late-at-night dark. I can see the stars. I hadn't even noticed them.

"You're asleep," I say, and then feel stupid for stating the obvious. "Never mind. This was—I shouldn't have called you. I'm sorry."

"Dani?"

"Yeah."

"I thought it was you." He sounds a little more awake now. "Where are you?"

"At the house. Mom's asleep and I'm . . . I just thought I'd call. At"—I squint at a window, catch a glimpse of the clock by the television—"four in the morning. I didn't realize it's so late. I'm sorry."

"Don't be. Let me just—ow!" I hear the sound of something falling. "Um, pretend you didn't hear that."

"Are you all right?"

"Fine. I just—I fell out of bed."

I laugh and can practically hear him smile over the phone when he says, "I should have known that would cheer you up."

"Well, it was pretty funny . . . wait a second. How did you know it was me?"

"You didn't say hello, just started talking. Very you. Plus I would know your voice anywhere."

I don't know what to say to that. It turns out I don't have to say anything because he says, "I'll see you soon, okay?"

"Okay."

After I hang up I go back inside to check on Mom. She's asleep. She looks . . . she looks like she always does. But then, as I'm leaving her room, I see the bottles of pills the doctor prescribed on her dresser. He wasn't happy when I told him I was going to take her somewhere else, started talking about time again, but from somewhere deep inside, from a place

I didn't know I had, I found this voice. A strong voice, a sure one.

I told him I understood, but that I had to think of my mother first. I asked him questions, all the ones I'd wanted to before and hadn't. I asked about other places: other hospitals, other doctors. He told me things, gave me numbers to call. He shook my hand when I got up to leave. He said he wished me all the best. I believed him.

I arranged for Mom to be released. I tried to talk about our options on the way home. She said she was tired and that we'd have to talk later. I made phone calls while she slept. When she woke up, she said she was going out for a while.

"Are you coming back?"

She looked at me. She looked at the lists I'd written. She looked out the window at the car, at the driveway leading to the road.

"Yes," she said, quietly, and I believed her.

She came back but still didn't want to talk. "I'm tired," she said again. "I'm so tired." It was then I realized what she'd done, where she'd been.

She'd been to the houses. She'd gone and looked at them, dreamed of what was inside. She had to do it because they're her world, her life. She'd gone because she needs them.

"We'll talk in the morning," I said, and pretended I didn't see the sorrow on her face.

After that I just sat. I sat downstairs, in the dark, and then I went outside and called Greg. I know why I called him.

I want to see him.

I'm still thinking about that when he shows up. I watch his car come down the driveway. The lights make my eyes hurt. He turns them off and everything is dark again. I hear him get out of the car. I sit on the steps. I hear him walking toward me.

"Hey," he says, and I see him right in front of me, a dark shape against a backdrop of night sky and sea. "What's going on?"

"Nothing."

He sits down next to me. "Is that your way of saying you just wanted to see how I look at four thirty in the morning?"

I glance over at him and he's grinning. I see the flash of his teeth. There are a lot of things I could say, but I just tell him the truth.

"I—I wanted to see you."

"That's good, 'cause I wanted to see you too. I've been wondering how you are. And how's your mom? I heard about the—I heard she had to go to the hospital."

I tell him everything. He doesn't say a word, just listens, and when I'm done talking we sit there, silent, for a long while.

"How do you feel?" he asks when the sun is starting to rise, coloring the bottom of the sky brilliant, impossible colors.

"Angry. Scared. She doesn't seem to care. Not about anything the doctor said, not about treatment, not about—not about anything."

"Maybe she's scared too."

"She's never scared."

"Everyone gets scared." He looks at me. "Watch, I'm going to get scared right now. You ready? You sure? Okay." He takes a deep breath. "Pretty much anywhere you go, they're always looking for cops."

"Being able to get a job anywhere is scary? Why would that—?"

He moves toward me, closing the space between us. "Dani," he says quietly, and I realize what he meant.

"Oh. But you and me, we aren't—haven't—"

He smiles. "I know. I'm just saying. Just . . . putting it out there. A possibility because I—" He clears his throat. "You know, we're not so different, you and I."

"What?"

"I suppose I should be happy I've gotten you back to questions." He bumps his shoulder against mine. "I just—I think we have a lot in common."

"You and me?"

"No, the other two people sitting here."

"You're a cop."

"Yep."

"I'm a . . ."

"I know."

I look down at the ground. "It's all I know. And being something else, doing something else, I don't know how—I can't—"

"You can do anything."

No one has ever said anything like that to me before, and looking at him I think that maybe, just maybe, he could be right. Maybe I can. "Why did you say that?"

"Because I believe it. And because I really like you. There, I said it. I really like you. I want to get to know you."

"Me?"

He gives me a look.

"But why?"

"Because when I first saw you I thought—no, I knew—you were special. Because I still think that every time I look at you. Because I think you're smart and funny and brave. But most of all"—he grins at me—"because I like questions."

"But I steal things."

"So stop."

"It's not—it's not like that. Not that easy."

"Yeah," he says, "it is. You're not doing it now, are you?" I laugh and he says, "See? Not so hard."

"But people like me—"

He leans toward me, and whatever I thought I was going to say dries up and flies away, lost in his eyes. In what I see in them.

"Dani," he says, and then he kisses me.

He kisses me and I kiss him back and when we separate I feel like the whole world has tilted sideways. I feel like I'm seeing it for the very first time.

I smile at him, and watch as he smiles back.

"You know who you are," he says. "You just have to believe it."

33

For the first time ever, I pick where we go. Where we are. Mom didn't want to choose or even think about it. She just shook her head when I asked and then closed her eyes. I listed choices anyway. She didn't respond. She was pretending to be asleep but in a few minutes she actually was. She tires easily these days, though she won't admit it.

We could have flown but Mom wanted to drive. It was the only thing she asked for, the only thing she said when I told her where we were going. I had to buy maps, which I knew how to do, and then I had to get my license. That I didn't know how to do. I'd only ever had ones that didn't belong to me.

I went in expecting to wait in line, sit for an awful picture, and then walk back out. It turned out there's a test. It was the first one I've ever taken. I passed and left with my very own driver's license. It's strange to look down and see my name, my real name, on it.

I know a lot about cancer now. I know what metastasized means; I know what the drugs Mom takes are supposed to do. I know a shadow on a lung can mean nothing or it can mean a doctor looking at the floor and then looking at you, sorrow on his face.

The doctor mostly talks to me when the two of us are in his office, probably because I ask a lot of questions but maybe because I write the checks that pay him. Mom makes him laugh though, and she's the one who found out he has two kids in boarding school, that they both need braces, and that every summer he takes his entire family to an island off the coast of Georgia. She asked me to buy her a map of Georgia the other day and I did, watched her look at it while she sat through chemo.

"It's not that far away," she said, and turned the map so I could see it, her fingers marking the island. Both of us pretended we didn't notice the IV dug deep into her arm, the tube coming out of it. "A day's drive."

"And a boat ride."

Mom laughed and then folded the map, handed it

to me. "You hold on to it."

I have. I am. I keep it by the window next to the plant I bought last week. I've never had a plant before. It's not a dog, but I figure it's best to start slowly.

Mom is staying in a hotel. It's really nice, the kind of place we always stayed in when things were going well. She has a big room, a beautiful view, a maid coming in and turning down the beds every night. When I told her I was going to find a place of my own she looked at me like I was crazy and gestured around the room. "You have a place."

"A real place."

Mom turned away from me, stared out the window. "This is real."

I took a deep breath. "I want to do this."

She was silent for a long time, and then she turned and looked at me.

"Baby," she finally said, "don't expect me to come with you."

I hadn't, but it still hurt when she said it.

One of the nurses who works chemo helped me find my apartment. Her brother was moving to Kansas and needed to sublet his place. She told me that when

I was looking through the classifieds, wrote her brother's phone number down on top of the paper after she hooked Mom's IV into place. I sat with the paper folded in my lap after she walked off, looking down at it and listening to the slow harsh sound of Mom breathing.

"You should call."

I looked up. Mom was staring at her IV.

"I can wait."

Mom looked at me. "Someone who wants to sublet won't ask questions like a landlord will. No credit check, no background check . . ."

I got up and made the call. When I came back Mom was reading a magazine. She handed it to me. "Quiz me."

I did. She was an "all or nothing kind of gal." She smiled when I told her that. The nurse came by and said the IV was looking good.

"So, this apartment," Mom said to her. "What's the neighborhood like?"

"Oh, it's perfectly safe. Right by the university. I have two little ones myself, and I know how it is. You want to make sure your children are taken care of."

"That's right. And thanks to you, she's got a good place. Now all she needs is a millionaire husband. I don't suppose you know where she could get one of those."

The nurse laughed and told us about a neighborhood on the far west side of the city. "You should see the houses. A new museum wing"—she gestured at the newspaper on the floor—"was just donated by someone who lives out there."

"Oh, I read about that," Mom said, and looked at me. "Baby, when we're done here, let's go for a drive, okay?"

"Okay," I said, and tried to want what I knew was coming.

I couldn't.

We went for our drive. I saw Mom sit up straighter when we finally reached a neighborhood that called to her. I watched her look out the window at the houses. I saw how happy they made her.

I took her to see my apartment the next day. She waited while I talked to the guy, charmed him when he spoke to her. She watched him hand me the keys. She came in, looked around.

"You're really doing this."

"Yes."

"Nice view," she said. "Can you take me back to the hotel?"

I did. She hasn't unpacked her bags yet. I don't think she ever will.

I've thrown mine away. I bought a dresser last week at a thrift store. It's old and the drawers are warped and it leans a little to one side, but it's mine for as long as I want. For forever if I choose. I keep my books on top of it.

I'm still getting used to the school thing. I thought signing up for GED classes would be a big deal but it wasn't. I just went and did it. Just like that. I don't mind the homework, but talking in class is weird. I'm used to being silent, blending in, only saying what I'm supposed to. It seems strange to be asked to give my opinion on a book or what happened to some long-dead president hundreds of years ago. I kind of like it, even if I do have a lot to learn.

Everyone in class calls me Dani. I really like that. The girl who sits next to me says I'm lucky because I never went to high school. Her name is Rachel and she works at a sandwich place in what everyone around here calls "The Fan."

The sandwich place is pretty cool. The owner, Maureen, is into art and is always having exhibits of stuff made by university students. She says she hired me because I'm the only person who ever asked what the statue on her desk in the back is supposed to be. She says I have a creative mind.

Mom was mad about the job. I told her about it after chemo one afternoon, when we were driving down a wide tree-lined street through the only neighborhood that seemed to bring her any joy. She was looking at houses, one hand pressed against the window, but she turned to look at me after I finished talking.

"A job?"

I nodded and I knew from her voice I definitely wasn't going to be telling her about school yet.

"You got a job," she repeated. "Why?"

"I wanted to."

"Pull over."

I did and she reached over, turned the car off, and took the keys.

"Baby," she said. "Look at me. This house—" She gestured around us. All I could see was the street and a security fence. "This house is maybe worth concentrating on. Maybe. But it's just one place and there are others out there. Better places. Better things. You know that."

"Maybe I don't want better."

She turned toward me. I saw so many things on her face. Disappointment. Fear. Love.

"I know I'm going to die."

"Mom—"

"I am. You talk to the doctor, baby, but I watch his face. I watch his hands. He always taps the desk when he talks about my future. You see my hands?" She held them out toward me. "They're still. They're still because I know what to do with them. The doctor doesn't, not when he's talking about me, and we both know why."

"You don't know that. You—"

"Stop. Listen. I know, and you do too. And I want more for you than this when I'm gone. I want more for you than what I had when I was your age. I taught you everything I know, and there's nothing in this world you can't do. Nothing."

"I know," I said, and watched my mother's face fall.

We sat in silence for a long time. Finally she handed me the car keys.

"I'm sorry," I told her.

"No," she said. "You aren't."

She's right. I'm not sorry for the choices I've made. I see her in me now, finally, in how I've made up my mind and am moving forward. I get up in the mornings and make sandwiches. I study. I take Mom to chemo. I ask the doctor questions, do research at the library, and come back with more questions. I go to school. I walk by the university and think that maybe someday I could be there.

I visit Mom at the hotel and watch television with her. She's met a businessman. He brings clients to the hotel, takes them out to eat in the restaurant. He says it impresses them and his clients always want to be impressed. He sells real estate. He's offered to take her to see one of the houses he's trying to sell this weekend.

"You'll be careful?" I ask, and hand her a glass of juice. She has a hard time eating or drinking after chemo. It leaves a funny taste in her mouth. She says it never goes away.

"Don't worry about me." She takes the glass. The

sun shines in through the window, dances through her hair. It is still dark and full, beautiful. The nurses tell her she's lucky. Mom always smiles and says she guesses she is.

"I can't help it."

"I know." She takes a sip, grimaces, and then puts the cup down. "But you don't need to."

"I know," I echo, and lean over, rest my head on her shoulder. She changes the channel, kisses the top of my head, and then moves away, sinking into the pillows with a yawn. I watch her lying there, perfectly still with her eyes closed, and then I get up and rinse out the juice glass. I stand watching water spill out of it and rush down the sink for a long time. When I go back to the bed, I cover her with a blanket, tucking it around her.

"I love you," I whisper. Her face twitches, but she stays still, stays silent. I grab my stuff and leave, go to class. Rachel asks me if I want to take over her shift tomorrow morning. I say I do.

"What are you going to do?" Mom asks when we're sitting in the hospital waiting room one afternoon. She's thinner now, frailer. She no longer wants me to sit with her during chemo. She says some things are easier on her own.

I know what she's really asking. I know what she wants the answer to be, and part of me wants to tell her what she wants to hear. She raised me to live a certain way, to believe in certain things.

"Go to school," I tell her. "That's what I'm going to do. That's what I am doing."

"School? After everything you've seen and done, everything you know, you want to go to school? What can school teach you?"

"I don't know." I look at her and smile. "I guess I'll learn."

She doesn't smile back. "You should want more."

I lean over, rest my hand on top of hers. "I'm happy."

She shakes her head but doesn't pull away. When the nurse comes to get her she says, "You don't have to wait, you know."

"I know. I want to."

I read magazines after she's gone. There aren't any new ones yet so I read the ones Mom and I have read before. I take a quiz she once did. I'm starting to add up my answers when I hear a voice ask where the waiting room is. I look up.

Through the glass doors I see Greg approaching. His hair has grown out to the crazy stage again, but even without it I'd still know him anywhere. I sent a postcard to him at the police station last week, a picture of a sculpture I saw in the museum. I didn't have to go to the museum for school or anything. I just thought it would be interesting to go. It was.

The sculpture I saw looked like nothing from far away, just a lump of rock, but up close you could see it was a figure pushing up out of the ground and reaching toward the sky. There was a little plaque under it. It said "Stealing Heaven." I looked at it for a long time. On the back of the postcard I wrote the hospital name and then my own. Dani. Just that, and nothing more.

My mother taught me to believe in silver, to believe in things, but I think it's more important to believe in me.

Elizabeth Scott grew up in a town so small it didn't even have a post office, though it did boast an impressive cattle population. She's sold hardware and panty hose and had a memorable three-day stint in the dot-com industry, where she learned that she really didn't want a career burning CDs. She lives just outside Washington, DC, with her husband; firmly believes you can never own too many books; and would love it if you visited her website, www.elizabethwrites.com.